THE GUIN SAGA

Book Five: The Marches King

KAORU KURIMOTO

TRANSLATED BY ALEXANDER O. SMITH

WITH ELYE J. ALEXANDER

VERTICAL.

Yuri Igarashi Alexander and Benjamin J. Alexander contributed to the translation.

Published by Vertical, Inc., New York.

Originally published in Japanese as *Henkyo no Oja* by Hayakawa Shobo, Tokyo, 1980.

ISBN 978-1-934287-20-0

Manufactured in the United States of America

First Edition

Vertical, Inc.
1185 Avenue of the Americas 32nd Floor
New York, NY 10036
www.vertical-inc.com

Guin, the leopard-headed warrior. When he appeared in the Roodwood he was but a wanderer, utterly alone. Now he had friends, the Lagon and the Sem.

—The Chronicles of Cheironia

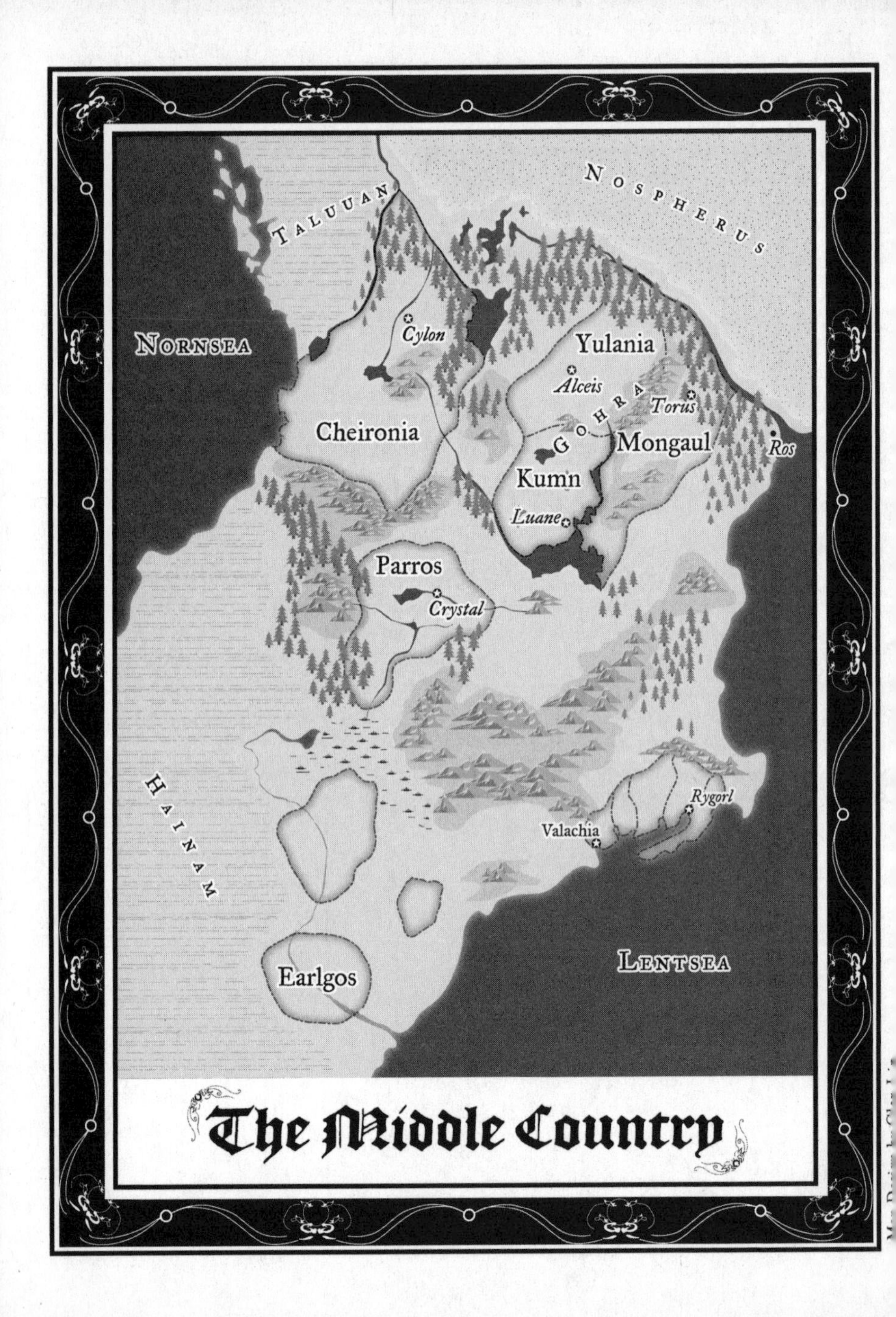

NOSPHERUS
TALUUAN
NORNSEA
Cylon
Yulania
Alceis
GOHRA
Torus
Ros
Cheironia
Mongaul
Kumn
Luane
Parros
Crystal
HAINAM
Rygorl
Valachia
LENTSEA
Earlgos
The Middle Country

CONTENTS

Dog's Head
Mountain
Devil Rock
Karoi Valley
Raku Valley
N O S P H E R U S
The Devil's Anvil
Stafolos
The River Kes
Mongaul
Alvon
N

Chapter One

Lagon Rising

— I —

Drip...

A drop of ice-cold water fell.

The water had been dripping at slow but regular intervals for some time now. It was a vexing sound that pricked the ears and frayed the nerves.

Drip...

The droplet struck a rock, ran across its surface. Over time the falling water had begun to fill the cracks that spread across the hard pale ground, overflowing to puddle in the low places. In the dim light, the ground shone with surprising brightness, like an eye glistening with tears. Yes, dampness, water gathering—but it would never reach him.

Drip...

Guin had been sitting, hunched and motionless, listening, waiting for each drop to fall in turn, for some time now. All that water, and not a drop for him.

To chain a man to a rock so close to water that he might touch it if only he could extend a hand, lick the moisture with his tongue if only he could lean forward—surely, there is no better means to drive a prisoner mad, to weaken him, to bring him to Death's threshold—no surer, more reliable method to torture a soul. Yet it was unclear how thoroughly the ones who had chained him there had thought out their plan, whether they had measured his chains when they placed him in that hole in the rock.

What was certain was that Guin was terribly thirsty. He wished, now, that he had not tasted the rock salt in that beautiful, white valley filled with death where he had met his captors.

Guin did not curse his circumstances or rage against his chains. He knew it would do no good; he also knew that protesting would show weakness to those who had placed him there. And so he sat, silently and still, without moving for several twists. With his feline head hung low over his chest, the half-man, half-beast stretched out his long legs and leaned up against the rock behind him, resting his body as best he could. He gave no outward sign of his fierce and growing frustration.

Again, almost mockingly: *Drip...*

In this rocky hollow untouched by morning, noon, or night, it was impossible for Guin to tell just how much time had passed since he came through the valley of white salt, met the four Lagon, and became their prisoner. It might have been a moment, or a half-day, or even an entire cycle of the sun. No one had brought him food, which meant that either not enough time had passed for a meal to come, or his captors simply did not deign to feed their monstrous charge.

Crouched in the darkness as he was, his golden eyes staring into the gloom, he felt that the very flow of time had lost its precision and meaning until it became something fluid, stretching and contracting like some black, insidious amoeba.

Yet Guin could not afford to let himself float in such uncertainty, to linger without taking action. He had come to these mountains, far across the desert, to ask the barbarian Lagon if they would join the Sem in fighting against a danger that threatened all who called Nospherus home—and he had only been given four days in which to do it.

If the four days ran out without word from Guin, the Sem fully intended to kill the hostages he had left behind: Princess Rinda and Prince Remus, the orphans of Parros. If he did not return, they would consider it a betrayal, branding him a coward who ran to save his own skin rather than stand and fight.

Of course there was Loto, high chieftain of the Raku, whose granddaughter Suni had been saved by Guin and the twins of Parros. Loto would fight to protect Rinda and Remus, certainly. Yet there would be strong opposition—the strongest from Ilateli of the Guro tribe—and though Guin did not doubt for a moment the success of his strategy to use the mercenary Istavan to force the Karoi tribe into joining the struggle, their chieftain, Gaulo, was as violent and as bloodthirsty as Ilateli and would surely also demand retribution if he suspected a betrayal. It only made matters worse that the Karoi were given to thinking of the peaceful Raku as brown-furred cowards.

Only the *yidoh*-herding Tubai and the Rasa, blood-kin to the Raku, were likely to side with Loto should a confrontation arise. But if the worst should happen, and the Raku, Tubai, and Rasa were forced to join against the combined forces of the Guro and the Karoi, they would be overwhelmed. The Guro and the Karoi, the traditional warrior clans of the Sem, aggressive and wild by nature, were also physically larger and stronger than the other wildlings. The mild-mannered Raku and Rasa wouldn't stand a chance.

Guin just needed a little more time. Even if, by the time he returned, the Sem had split over whether or not to kill the twins, he felt confident that he could avert bloodshed and reconcile the tribes so long as he reached them before the fighting started. Then he could lead them to victory against their true enemy—or at least, that was what he hoped. So he sat, and thought, and waited.

The Sem were something very close to primitive humans:

brave, and possessing the first rudiments of culture, yet unable to grapple with abstract concepts or complex ideas. Strategy, foresight, long-term calculations—not even the great Loto, considered a sage among his people, understood these things except in a vague and simple way. The minds of the Sem, like their bodies, resembled those of human children. Thus it had mystified them when Guin departed to ask for help from the Lagon giants when the Sem still had the upper hand in Nospherus, and the more suspicious among them had feared that their Riyaad, their prophesied leader, was abandoning them.

They did not understand why they had won every battle they had fought against the Mongauli army, even against numbers several times their own, nor how they had managed to turn every disadvantage into an advantage. They scarcely comprehended the scope of Guin's efforts: the use of the hideous yidoh, the clever decoy, the calling to arms of the Karoi, and the near total destruction of all two thousand of Count Marus's blue knights. It had been enough for the little wildlings to mindlessly follow their leopard-headed champion, and so they had done faithfully, claiming victory again and again. It had never occurred to them to wonder why. They followed Guin because they saw him win, and trusted him to win again.

Yet had Guin failed even once, they would have ceased to

follow him as swiftly as a dust-devil coils and fades in the Nospherus sun. "We Sem have our own way of fighting," they would say, forgetting all that had passed. "Why rely on the help of a stranger?" From the very beginning, Guin was walking on a tight rope above a valley of shining blades. He had come this far without fault, but there was no guarantee that his next step would not be his last.

He had no choice but to walk on.

Now he sat in the dark, listening to the *drip, drip, drip* of the water, muttering to himself in a low growl.

He had made it this far. What good would it do to pause and quail, gazing at the taut rope ahead of him now? Even if he had to inch forward, clutching the rope with both hands, it would be progress. After all, no matter how grim his present situation, he was better off than when he had first appeared in the Roodwood, where his memory began.

Then he had been as one newly born, without a scrap of armor to protect him or an inkling of where he was, deep in an unknown forest rife with man-eating ghouls and hostile Mongauli knights. At that perilous awakening Guin had known only his name, and one other word—"Aurra"—its meaning as mysterious as his own identity. He was naked, bloodied, and freakish, with the head of a beast where the face of a man should have been. So he had been born, a twisted orphan of the Roodwood.

Shortly thereafter he had saved the twins of Parros from the knights of Stafolos Keep, more out of basic instinct than any conscious decision. Yet that act had set the wheel of his fate into motion, and soon he and the twins had become prisoners of the keep, only to escape when a night raid by the Karoi left Stafolos in flames. Together with a sellsword, Istavan of Valachia, and the little Sem girl Suni, the companions had set off down the Kes River on a raft, outrunning their pursuers from Alvon Keep and fleeing into the wilds of Nospherus. So he had run as a fugitive, not knowing why he had to be chased, and fighting simply to survive, until, at last, he found friends worth fighting for, the wildling Sem.

How differently the path of Guin's days might have run had he encountered not the tiny desert denizens but a modern, mounted force, skilled in strategy, such as the armies of another of the kingdoms in the Middle Country, or the resistance forces desperately struggling to rebuild conquered Parros. Yet he thought not of what might have been, but of what was. He had been given the Sem, and the yidoh. He had been given Nospherus. That was all he had, and he was determined to do everything in his power to protect it from the Mongauli forces. Fate had dealt him his hand; it was up to him to play the cards.

Now another disturbing possibility occurred to him. What if, even before the Sem had the chance to execute the twins or fall into the tribal strife a stay of execution would surely entail, they were preemptively attacked by the Mongauli army? The four days he had requested from the Sem were more than just the amount of time he expected their trust in him to last. It was also the limit after which the various steps he had taken to ensure the Sem's superiority in Nospherus would cease to become effective.

If anything occurred that he had not foreseen, or any of his carefully made calculations had been in error, all his effort would evaporate like the morning dew on the Nospherus sands.

In any case he only had two days from the time when the Lagon had captured him until his time was up. How many hours had passed since then? If a whole day had indeed gone by while he sat there chained to the rock, then only a day remained. And if, outside, the second day's sun was already creeping toward the horizon, then the gambit was over, and he had lost.

Yet there was nothing he could do. There had been no opportunity to attempt wooing the Lagon with words. He was stuck in a rocky prison, all the giants out of earshot. And even if his luck changed this instant and the Lagon set him free and agreed to march to war at his side, there must be preparations for battle, and then the long journey back over the Dog's Head. Indeed, the likeliest outcome of this adventure, even should he manage to win over his captors, was that they would not arrive in time to save the Sem or the royal twins.

If only he had access to the secret of Parros that had enabled Rinda and Remus to escape the burning Crystal Palace and journey with lightning swiftness to the Roodwood, far, far away! If he knew the workings of that ancient mechanism then it would be a simple affair to bring the Lagon armies right before the Mongauli in an instant—but this was an empty dream. *Ah, Rinda, Remus, if only you knew how valuable you are! Your worth is greater than a thousand times your weight in diamonds. So precious you are that an entire army has gone mad trying to claim you.* If the Mongauli could capture the twins, and through them the secret of Parros, then they would conquer not only the Middle Country, but the entire world.

Enough.

Guin lifted his head, pushing these thoughts from his mind. Some things it was better not to waste time pondering. He might be surrounded by enemies, and plunged into what was, by any reckoning, an entirely hopeless situation, but he had no intention of giving up and leaving his fate in the hands of the gods, for that was the coward's way. If there came a day when the twins of Parros breathed their last, all the tribes of the Sem slaughtered down to the last brave warrior and a sword thrust through his own neck, that—and not a moment sooner—would be the day Guin stopped fighting.

Drip...

How could a simple sound be more maddening even than his thirst, or the hopelessness of his predicament? Wrapped in shadow, Guin swallowed his exasperation at the cruel workings of fate, forced down the bitter unease, and sat still as the rock around him.

Exerting his iron will, Guin wrenched his thoughts away from the burning thirst in his throat and considered the barbarians who had chained him there. Little was known about these giants of legend. Guin was likely the first man to have stepped within the borders of their territory in centuries, even millenia. The Lagon, together with the even more primitive Sem, were the only two peoples to live in this accursed land of Nospherus. Yet though their home was the same, how different they were!

Compared to the simian Sem, who stood only one *taal* in height and weighed no more than a ten-year-old human child, the Lagon were truly giants. The tallest among them stood two-and-a-half *taal* high, and weighed as much as a foal of three years. Though similarly covered in thick hair, the Lagon lacked the tails sported by the lesser wildlings, while that hair, veritable manes, coiled from the napes of their necks to their thick waists.

And compared to the Sem, whose capability for thought

had halted at a level that was decidedly pre-human, the Lagon appeared to possess something akin to intelligence. Though their faces were fearsome to behold, their eyes burned bright as lamps with the fires of a wild intelligence.

Guin had seen the giants' purpose in coming to the white valley where they captured him: they were there to harvest the rock salt. Sem cuisine was simple at best; they boiled the occasional root that was too hard to gnaw, but in essence they were hunter-gatherers who lived on the raw spoils of the wild land around them. Yet the Lagon gathered the seasoning stone, salt, and very likely used it to preserve their food. They even appeared to use the salt as a means of commerce. Guin knew this because as they hauled him to their village, he had asked them what their business was in the valley, and they had laughed at his ignorance.

"The white sand is sacred to *lagon*. The blessing of the white sand keeps away the earth-rot."

"The white sand can be traded for many things," another had said. "The little *lagon* come often hoping for a handful."

"Little *lagon*?" Guin had asked. "You mean the Sem?"

"Not *sem*. Your un-knowledge is vast, *lagon* who wears the head of a beast. Sem are not *lagon*, they are *sem*. Beasts of the sands. The little *lagon* of which we speak call themselves *kitai*."

Somehow when the Lagon spoke the word *sem*, Guin knew

that, in their language, it meant "ape." Yet he could not help but be astonished at his informant's next revelation. "The Kitai?"

So men from the land of Kitai had traveled across the mountains from the far side of Nospherus, entering the desert land from its eastern border, to trade with the Lagon. While the men of the Middle Country wrote off the far desolate reaches of this desert waste as the edge of the world and busied themselves conquering their own neighbors, the Kitai, who were a familiar sight in any land with a trading port, had opened routes into these outer marches and conceivably might soon enter Nospherus, perhaps even crossing the Kes to arrive at the three archduchies of Gohra.

Guin had always suspected there was some reason that Mongaul had turned its eyes toward Nospherus. Perhaps it was, ultimately, to open trade routes—and perhaps the Mongauli were already too late. It would have been only one of their many miscalculations. A force of fifteen thousand men must have seemed a more than sufficient number to crush what little resistance the desert monkeys, barbarous giants, mindless yidoh, and vile sand leeches could offer. To an elite army, the wasteland no doubt had appeared to promise an easy conquest with scarcely the need to bloody a blade.

Obviously the Mongauli didn't know Nospherus.

It occurred to Guin that, at some point in the not too distant future, all eyes in all lands would turn to this barren borderland. Something lay hidden in Nospherus, and when that something came to light, every country in the known world, from the three archduchies of Gohra to Kitai on Nospherus's eastern border, and the ancient kingdom of Hainam whose ruler claimed to be descended from the royal line of Kanan itself, all the way to the shadow-bound theocracy of Ferah-la, would rush to be first to claim the prize.

Of course, this was merely conjecture. For the time being, Nospherus was, to most of the inhabitants of these lands, nothing more than a featureless stretch on a map, a strip of unknown territory dividing the eastern reaches of the world from the west.

The Lagon village to which Guin had been taken was situated in the mountains, not far from the valley of salt. Legends told that the Lagon never lingered in one place, but traveled constantly in the nomadic fashion. Other legends claimed that the mysterious race dwelt in the ruins of the empire that once reigned from deep in the Kanan mountain range, as eternal wards of the ancient relics.

When at last Guin met the fabled giants, he had discovered that both these legends were true, and at the same time, both were wrong.

The village of the Lagon was indeed nestled deep in the Kanan Mountains, but when Guin was brought through its midst, feeling the curious stares of the giants upon him, he had come away with the impression that this was not the ancestral home of the Lagon but simply one of many temporary communities they had made over the centuries.

Nonetheless, the village was an impressive sight. The giants' relatively advanced culture was clearly evident in the construction of their homes—not the simple pit dwellings of the Sem, but real houses built from blocks of rock hewn from the mountainsides. These stone houses were dark and cool within, and several of them seemed to serve the function of communal storehouses in which salted meat and rock amaranth could be stored. This alone proved that the Lagon possessed knowledge far exceeding that of the Sem.

It was only from subtle clues—an instinctual impression that Guin would have found hard to articulate—that the leopard-man guessed that the Lagon had come here relatively recently, and that they likely relocated at regular intervals, carving the mountain stone to build new villages like this one where they would live for years, or possibly decades, before packing up and moving on again.

Perhaps this strategy was designed to obscure the location of their homes from the great desert wolves and from the Sem, and was furthermore a convenient way to gain access to new pastures and hunting grounds. Though they knew methods for storing food, they did not yet seem to have discovered the art of cultivating the soil. Even had they been so inclined, there was little arable land in these rugged mountains or the surrounding desert on which to grow even the hardiest crop.

Apparently the Lagon represented a step in civilization between that of the Sem and that of the peoples of the Middle Country and the far east. Though they did not yet practice agriculture, they were beginning to wean themselves from the nomadic hunting life.

Yet the language they spoke was very similar to that of the Sem. Guin wondered just how the tiny Sem and the giant Lagon had diverged into what they were today. And what to make of the unbelievable claims that both Sem and Lagon were children of the ancient Kanan Empire—in other words, descended from humans? What demon's hands had twisted them into their current form? *Nospherus, Nospherus...* Though his thoughts wandered they always came back to this harsh land. If only he could understand these peoples, if he could unravel their mysteries, he might uncover the deeper mystery that lay hidden in its sands.

Like the secret of the ancient machinery of Parros, this land, too, held a secret that could change the world.

How could men like myself become Lagon, or Sem, falling so far?

Guin stiffened, as though an icy hand had grasped his heart.

Men like myself? Am I a man? They called me the lagon who wears the head of a beast. Then what am I? Am I human? Am I—

A low growl, released at last after long hours of tortured self-control, escaped from between Guin's huge fangs. Suddenly, he reached up to seize his leopard-masked head as forcefully as the chains would allow him, and shook it wildly as if he had gone mad.

Then, just as abruptly, he stopped.

Guin lowered his hands and glared out into the darkness.

Someone was watching him.

2

"Ah!"

With a small yelp of surprise, the unknown watcher froze outside the rough-cut window of Guin's cell. The leopard-man had initially assumed it was one of his captors—a warden, perhaps—come to check on him, but now he wondered if it might be some newcomer among the giants come to see the strange prisoner with the head of a beast. What had caught his attention in the gloom of the cave were two orbs burning with a yellow flame, like the fearsome eyes of a wild animal in the darkness.

Guin stifled the growl rising in his throat, and fixed his gleaming eyes on his visitor.

Gradually he made out the form of a small Lagon—a child, in fact. The youngster was nearly the size of an ordinary human man—tall enough that his head would be even with Guin's chest if the leopard-warrior were standing. Yet the way he leaned up against the edge of the window suggested that unbalanced quality that children of all races share; and his eager, childlike curiosity was palpable.

The youngster's face was slender for a Lagon's, and topped with long hair, thick and tangled, much of it black with dirt and caked mud. Yet his trembling eyes were filled with the innocence of a newborn calf.

The young Lagon stared warily at the captive. He seemed on the verge of shouting and running for his life, yet Guin's powerful gaze held him like a magnet, and the youngster stood frozen, as though caught in some ensorcelment.

"A...Amu," he said, his voice shaking as he made a visible effort to stop trembling. The youngster was terribly nervous, that much was clear. Guin averted his harrowing gaze, and his visitor immediately seemed to relax. After a moment the visitor turned from the window as if to leave, his curiosity satisfied.

"Lagon!" Guin called to his back. "Tell me, what time is it now?"

The Lagon jumped, then froze in place. Guin's eyes held him fixed, and the leopard-man's voice, accustomed to giving orders, was persuasive as a whip. The Lagon child had no choice but to respond.

"A...Aii." After a moment's hesitation, he turned. Obviously he could not see well into the darkness of the prison cave. Yet he stood, staring through the window, meeting Guin's bright eyes. "Aii... What...?"

"I asked you what time it is now. Lagon, do not leave." Guin spoke this time with even greater force.

The Lagon child stood immobile for a long moment. Then he edged closer to the window, peering more carefully inside. Perhaps he was relieved that the strange prisoner spoke his own wildling tongue. Guin flattened himself against the rock wall behind him. It would not do to show too much of his face to his visitor and scare him further. His voice softened, and he asked his question again.

His visitor replied, "What...time? I do not understand."

"You must know. Tell me."

"I do not understand."

Then it occurred to Guin that these Nospherus wildlings might have no system for dividing the day into periods that could be named or numbered. "Let me ask this, then: is the sun in the sky, or is it night? Does the moon shine upon the land?"

The Lagon furrowed his brow. "Yes, the sun is in the sky, where else would it be?"

"Is it high? Is it close to evening?"

"I do not know. Do not understand."

"The sky—is it red?"

"Your words, they make little sense. I think perhaps your head is strange," the Lagon said with something that sounded almost like a laugh. "Sky is blue. Sky is always not red."

"Well, I suppose it's not, I mean—Doalspit!—is the sky blue now, or is it black?"

"Blue."

"Since I came to this place, have you slept? How many times have you eaten?"

"Too early for sleep. *Lagon* sleep only at night. I ate two salt-meats," his young informant answered. Guin scratched at his chest. Now he was getting somewhere. At least it seemed that the sun had not yet set on the third day. That meant he was left with at least a day and a night.

Perhaps I have enough time after all.

"I have a request for you. Will you hear it?" Guin said earnestly.

"What? You are—you are evil, a *lagon* I have never seen. What if you are a demon? Mother told me never to listen to demons and their words."

"But you're listening now, aren't you?" Guin pointed out. "Well? Has any harm befallen you?"

"No," the youth said thoughtfully. "Nothing falls. No harm."

"See? I am no demon, I promise you this. Please, hear my request."

"What is it?"

"Bring me one of those saltmeats such as you ate. And something to drink."

"Meat, and water?"

For a moment, Guin thought his visitor would refuse, but after a long pause the youngster spoke again. "I will go to the foodhouse, and bring you meat." Then the Lagon turned and ran. Guin heard his footfalls receding down the hall.

A short while later, as the leopard-man sat deep in thought, he heard the thud of something thrown through the window landing on the stone floor of the cavern.

"Meat, I brought for you." The youth had returned, and his voice was high pitched with excitement. "Mother is big *lagon* at the food house. She gets much food—as much as we need."

"I thank you," Guin said. But there was still a problem. He was overjoyed that the youth had brought him food, but now the saltmeat was lying on the floor beneath the window, well out of his reach where he sat chained to the stone wall in the back of the room. "I'm bound to this rock and can't move. Bring a stick, and use it to push the meat to me, please."

It appeared that his friend was beginning to take interest in their exchange. To a curious child it must have seemed like a marvelous game. Guin had relied on this from the moment he saw that his visitor was a youngster. As long as Guin kept his interest up and didn't make him too uncomfortable, the Lagon child would probably do anything he asked.

After some time and a great deal of prodding with a long stick the Lagon had found, Guin held the meat in his hand. He doubled over, getting his head as close to his hand as he could, and crammed it laboriously through his mask into his mouth. It was terribly salty, being nothing more than raw meat caked with salt, but after long days of eating nothing but the plain food of the Sem, the taste alone was enough to breathe the life back into him.

Guin finished the sizable hunk of meat in the blink of an eye. He could have eaten more, but even this was enough to rejuvenate his strength and vastly improve his spirits. Yet his throat stung with thirst. He pleaded with his young friend for something to drink.

This did not turn out to be as easy as the meat. Yet, after a long search, the child was able to bring him a primitive canteen made of carved wood, with a cork in one end. When he pushed it over to the leopard-man it made a pleasant sloshing sound. Guin held the canteen between his knees, used his teeth to pry out the cork, and drank deeply. Ordinary water had never tasted so sweet, so delicious, nor had it ever felt so invigorating. In a moment he had drunk it all.

"Ahh..." Guin sighed, licking his lips like a contented lion. "May Janos repay your kindness a thousandfold! I won't forget what you have done for me. I feel like a man reborn." He thought for a moment. "Say, can you tell me, is this village of the Lagon large?"

"Of course," the child said, eyes wide, gazing in through the darkness at the strange man-beast hunched in the shadows. "The *lagon* are great and powerful," he declared with evident pride. "Dodok the Brave and Kah the Wise lead us true."

"And are Dodok the Brave and Kah the Wise in the village now?"

"Of course. As the sun and the moon are in the sky, they lead the Lagon. You know nothing."

"That's right, I don't. That's why I want you to teach me. Tell me about the Lagon. How many are you?"

"We are many, many," his young informant replied. Guin tried several times to elicit a specific number, but the answer was always the same. Either the Lagon were as poor with numbers as the Sem, or his informant was too young to have learned counting.

"Do the Lagon enjoy combat? Do they like to fight?"

"*Aii*... I do not understand."

"Are the Lagon strong?"

"*Lagon* are stronger than any other. Bhin stronger than Ta. Ran stronger than Bhin. Tii defeat Ran with one arm. And San and Ehb, and Lho are stronger than Tii, but Dodok the Brave strongest of all. He is the Brave. That is why Dodok the Brave is Dodok the Brave."

"I see," Guin said, collecting his thoughts. From what the child was saying, he could assume that the Lagon did enjoy combat, yet it seemed their militant energies were not directed at subduing other races, such as the Sem, but were exhausted vying for rank within their own community.

It sounded as though this Dodok the Brave were leading the Lagon together with Kah the Wise, yet he did not seem to be a hereditary chieftain in the vein of Loto, Ilateli, or Gaulo of the Sem, but rather the strongest warrior among the giants. He could picture a tournament whereby all the warriors would fight, with the winner of the final match claiming the title "brave" and leadership of the tribe.

If that were the case, Guin was in luck. All he had to do was to lure Dodok the Brave into combat. Even if the Lagon didn't immediately accept him as their leader, a victory should still earn him enough respect among these hulking warriors that organizing a force to aid the Sem would be far more simple. As for the prospect of doing combat with the strongest among the Lagon, Guin was confident in his chances. Though these creatures were giants even compared to him, they were not particularly massive for their height. After all, Guin had overcome the grey ape of Gabul, a head taller than him and broader and heavier by far.

"I wish to meet Dodok the Brave."

He heard a gasp outside the window.

"Why?" the child asked after some time.

"Why?" Guin echoed loudly. "Because I'm stronger than Dodok the Brave."

"You lie!" came a swift response. Guin could hear the tremble of fear in the child's high-pitched voice.

"It is no lie. Just tell Dodok that I wish to try him in combat. If he refuses, it is because he is afraid of me. Because he knows that if we fight, I will win."

"There is none stronger than Dodok. If Dodok loses, Dodok will no longer be Dodok. Dodok is always strongest," the Lagon said.

The logic was confused, but it appeared that Guin's guess had hit the mark. He nodded to himself, satisfied, and went on, "Then call Dodok. Bring him here. Tell him I wish this. If he will not accept my challenge, tell him that I am stronger than he, and I am the next, true Dodok. I crossed the desert and mountains to test his strength, to challenge him. Tell him this."

Another gasp. "Who..." the child began after a pause, "Who are you, *lagon* with the head of a beast?"

"My name is Guin," the leopard-man replied, burying the twinge of doubt that he felt at his own words deep inside.

Though he had forgotten everything about his life before the Roodwood, when the girl Rinda called him Guin, he had responded naturally, unconsciously, accepting it as his name. It had to be right. *I am Guin.*

The child turned to run, but Guin called to him one last time. "Wait, child! Your name?"

"Rh...Rhana."

"Good. Then, Rhana, do not forget to tell Dodok what I, Guin, the leopard-headed warrior, have said here."

Rhana sped away without another word. Guin was listening to his footfalls disappear into the distance when a realization struck him.

Not "his" footfalls, but "hers"? Rhana was clearly a girl's name. So the one who had given him food and water was a Lagon female. Guin smiled and gazed at the window of his cell. Then another, more sobering thought crossed his mind. *I hope Rhana has the courage to deliver my challenge to Dodok the Brave.*

Even if he ran the entire distance, Guin would need a full day and a night for the journey back to the Sem camp. That meant he had to get the Lagon on the move today and no later.

He hoped that Rhana would bring his message to Dodok and, in their fury at the leopard-headed monster's impudence, the giants would drag him out of the cell. Yet if Rhana feared to admit that she had been to the cell, the challenge would never be delivered, and all his effort would have been in vain—

Even while he sat there thinking, precious time was slipping away.

No matter. I will deal with what happens when it happens, Guin decided, *and make my next move when it becomes clear what that move should be.* Now, he needed to conserve his strength, and so the chained warrior stretched out and made himself as comfortable as he could on the rock and closed his eyes. His stomach was full, and the burning in his throat had eased. As unfavorable as his conditions were, they had vastly improved in a short amount of time.

What will come, will come. What will be, will be.

Like many battle-hardened warriors, Guin was capable of sleeping at any time and in any place, returning to full wakefulness in an instant at the first sign of trouble. Within moments he was breathing regularly and softly. Rhana did not return, nor did an angry Dodok the Brave storm into the stone cell. Beyond Guin's ken, high above the stony mountains, the sun began its slow arc down the sky.

"Rise! Rise, captive!"

Guin had awoken at the first sound of footsteps approaching down the corridor, long before the shouting started. Now he was feigning sleep to better gauge his visitors.

"He sleeps well!" one guard spat.

"Like a lazy beast," another said.

On cue, Guin's eyes snapped open. Three of the giant wildlings were standing in the cave before him. They carried stone-tipped spears in their hands and were naked save for hide loincloths tied about their waists.

"Dodok the Brave and Kah the Wise will see you now," one of them announced with some pomp, then crouched to undo the leopard-man's chains.

Guin was glad he had taken the precaution of hiding the canteen Rhana had given him in a nook in the rock where the guards would not see it.

The loosened chains fell to the stone floor. Surrounded by Lagon, Guin exited the small cell. His arms and legs tingled with receding numbness.

It seemed that Rhana had not managed to deliver her message to the chief, but there was little Guin could do about that. The stone of the dark hallway through which he passed was rough cut and damp with moisture. They passed through a doorless opening in one wall and he found himself abruptly outside.

It was a windy night. The stars seemed closer and more numerous than they had over the sands of the Nospherus desert. White Aeris shone in the sky above the jagged silhouette of a rocky peak. The moon, like a giant platinum disc, and the stars, scattered across the black drape of the night beyond the mountains' spine, had the kind of harsh cold beauty that graces only such places where not a single tree grows or wild shrub flowers.

"Come along, monster," one of the guards said, yanking Guin mercilessly in his wake. The prisoner followed without resisting.

As he was led along Guin gazed at the layout of the village, familiar from his passage through it earlier that day. The giants' community was arranged on levels cut into the sides of the mountains that enclosed the valley. It was impossible to traverse it without either climbing or descending at almost every step. Now they descended toward a large open space at the very bottom of the vale that Guin guessed must function like the communal grounds of the Sem village. There were simple steps cut into the rock around this gathering place where the Lagon could sit to participate in tribal meetings. Perhaps the open ground was also used for their tournaments or the settling of conflicts.

Guin could see clearly thanks to the bright shining moon. His feet stepped lightly down the rough-cut stone steps. The three Lagon guards escorted him in silence. From somewhere far beyond the rocky slopes, the sound of a desert wolf's howl came to them on the wind. It was a lonely sound.

As they passed each stone house, heads covered with thick hair peered out of doorways and windows, observing their progress. Guin caught glimpses of women carrying infants, as well as some Lagon he assumed must be very elderly from the grayish tint of their hair. In general, he found it very difficult to tell the female Lagon from the males. Those with newborns had breasts swollen for nursing and thus were easy to spot, but those without young children were flat-chested and as well muscled in their shoulders and arms as their male counterparts.

Most of them wore nothing but a solid coat of fur. To Guin's eye, accustomed to the diminutive Sem, their height was unnerving and their necks seemed short and thick. Beneath jutting heavy brows eyes tracked the strange captive in silence with a mixture of curiosity and enmity. Though some heads withdrew into the doorways after the prisoner and his escort had passed, many of the Lagon emerged from their homes and followed the quartet down the steps. Before long a procession had formed.

To a hidden observer it might have seemed like a scene from a reenactment of Cirenos' descent into Hell. It was a forboding and yet eerily comical sight: Guin, pushed and prodded by his three captors, making his way down the long rough stair to the stony clearing, trailed by a long shuffling line of curious Lagon. Several warriors were already sitting on the carved stone steps around the gathering place, waiting for their leader to pass judgment on their strange captive. No one spoke a word.

As Guin and his captors paused in the middle of the open place, the women and children who had followed behind them filed around to take seats behind the warriors on the steps. Guin cast his eyes about looking for Rhana but found no one resembling her among the children. He gave up and turned his attention to the Lagon warriors.

The three Lagon that had taken him from his cell now formed a watchful semicircle behind him, their spears held ready. Each one of them was a half-head taller than the leopard-man. The expressions on their craggy faces suggested a mixture of disdain for their captive and fear at his unusual appearance.

Guin raised his eyes to see that two chairs had been set at the edge of the clearing. A Lagon sat upon each chair.

In the right-hand chair was a Lagon of incredible age. Every hair on his body was white, and he was thin and bony to the point of emaciation, but the eyes beneath his bushy brows burned with an intense light. It had to be Kah the Wise. And sitting next to him—

Guin's eyes narrowed ever so slightly.

Even though the Lagon was sitting, the leopard-man could tell he was immense—the biggest of any Lagon he'd seen so far. Were the giant to stand, he would be sure to overtop Guin by a full head and a half. His girth was massive for a Lagon as well. His shoulders, arms, and chest were thick with muscles that ran like bands of steel, bulging through his rich body hair, and his hideous face seemed drawn from a child's nightmare.

This, without a doubt, was Dodok the Brave, strongest of the Lagon.

Guin would have to fight him.

And win.

— 3 —

"You."

When Kah the Wise spoke, it was slowly, as if in a dream.

"Who are you?"

His voice was thick and rasping, but the eyes that peered out from beneath his bushy white brows gleamed with intelligence.

Guin, who had been sizing up Dodok the Brave's considerable strength and girth, turned his gaze to the other leader of the Lagon. Kah's eyes met his, probing him with a deep curiosity.

"I am..."

The moment Guin opened his mouth to reply, a stir went through the Lagon. Though a few among them had already heard him speak, most were now seeing him for the first time and were astonished to find that this leopard-headed man—like a creature out of some myth—could speak their own tongue.

Dodok's gaze filled with surprise beneath his jutting brow.

Only Kah the Wise showed no sign of untoward alarm. Slowly, he tilted his head, lending an ear to Guin's words.

"My name is Guin. I am...a warrior, though I know not whence I came, nor the name of my land of birth."

"Guin? Why do you not know where you hail from? Who are you?" Kah repeated quietly. Guin frowned, uncertain where to begin.

"He knows not whence he comes!" a deep, dangerous voice thundered. It was Dodok the Brave. "It is because he is an evil spirit—a demon! Kah the Wise, he has come from the Land of the Dead to wreak vengeance upon *lagon*. It is certain."

Here and there, the Lagon muttered in agreement. Some merely nodded, while others shouted that such a creature did not deserve a trial, and should be killed on the spot.

Kah the Wise slowly lifted his right hand. Again, the Lagon fell silent. "You will tell us. Who are you?"

This time, Guin had an answer for him. "I am Guin. I came here under orders to lead the Lagon down the true path."

"Whose orders?" Kah asked swiftly.

"Heaven's."

"What is heaven?"

"It is the two-faced god Janos, who rules this world."

"This...Janos, we do not know this god," said the Lagon chieftain.

"And who determines how the Lagon should be? Who determines their fate, or the way they must live? Who makes all things in the world move, protecting the Lagon, and giving righteous judgment to you, Kah? Alphetto?"

"Alphetto?" Kah replied incredulously, disdain clear in his voice. "Alphetto! That is the mud-god of the Sem. He is the god of foul insects that walk the Land of the Dead—the maggots that infest the corpse of our world, the Sem. *Lagon* care nothing for Alphetto."

"Then what? Whom do the Lagon worship?"

"You speak of Aqrra," Kah replied solemnly. To Guin's astonishment, the moment he said that word, all the Lagon seated around the clearing lowered their heads as one. "Aqrra made *lagon*, Aqrra protects *lagon*. Aqrra is the beginning of all things. There are many gods upon the land. Yet only Aqrra made us. Aqrra belongs only to us." Then he began to chant in a monotone: "Aqrra is only of *lagon*, and *lagon* were made by Aqrra."

All the Lagon echoed the chant in a low voice.

"Then that's who sent me," said Guin. "This Aqrra, in my language he is known as Janos. I came here under orders from Aqrra."

"Aqrra is only Aqrra. Aqrra has no other name. Aqrra is known only to *lagon*, whom Aqrra has made, and no other,"

Kah said forcefully. Guin began to grow irritated. Above him, Aeris was already high in the sky. He had no time to waste debating theology.

"Nonetheless, I came here from Aqrra!" the leopard-man exclaimed, thrusting out his chest. "I'm a messenger from Aqrra!"

"Aqrra!" the Lagon shouted, another ripple passing through the crowd. Now Dodok the Brave stood, towering so high he seemed almost to touch the low-hanging clouds.

"Silence him! Cut out his tongue, and cure it with salt! He has profaned the sacred Aqrra. He came to steal precious white salt from *lagon*. He claims to be a messenger from Aqrra, yet he is a thieving demon. Kill him."

Cries of "Kill him, kill him!" erupted from the crowd. The Lagon thrust their fists into the air, shouting for blood.

"Silence!"

The voice of Kah the Wise rang across the clearing. His right hand slowly rose, and at once, the commotion settled. Guin looked at that raised hand, then blinked and counted: Kah the Wise had six fingers.

Perhaps this was a requirement for becoming a sage among these people, Guin surmised, momentarily forgetting the urgency of his predicament, until his thoughts were interrupted by Kah's ever-calm voice.

"Guin, Warrior with the Head of a Beast, Dodok the Brave has made mighty accusations against you. One, that you are a demon from the Land of the Dead come to wreak vengeance upon *lagon*. Two, that you steal salt from the sacred valley. Should these claims prove true, they are grave matters indeed. But if these claims are not true, then still you have committed a sin far graver than that of being a demon: to blaspheme the name of Aqrra is to *lagon* worse than stealing salt, or killing a man in his sleep. Can you explain your two trespasses here, before myself, Kah the Wise, and Dodok the Brave? Can you prove these words that have come from your mouth?"

"I can," Guin said, staring directly back at him, "...I think."

"Then do so. *Lagon* are fair, *lagon* are just. If you are true, then you have nothing to fear."

"Then I shall explain myself," Guin said, taking a half-step forward. For a moment, his three guards tensed to strike, yet when they saw that he intended no action, they resumed their statue-like vigil.

The moon slipped out from behind a cloud, lighting the village of stone. Guin had placed himself in the exact center of the open ground. Legs wide set, hands bound behind his back at the wrists, the warrior thrust out his chest, and the pale blue-white gaze of Aeris made his feline head and muscular body swim with wavering light, like a statue at the bottom of the sea.

"I can prove myself," Guin repeated, somewhat louder. Kah leaned forward in his chair, tilting an ear toward the captive. The warriors, women, and children of the Lagon had fallen quiet. No demon had ever been tried in the village clearing before, and they didn't want to miss a moment.

"Listen to my words," Guin began, "then decide whether to punish me or not. I know the Lagon to be fair. See me here now. I speak your words, and except for my beast-head, I share your form. Is my appearance cause enough to treat me as a demon? I do not think you are so barbarous as that. I believe in the Lagon."

"Yes, we are fair," came an undercurrent of voices in the crowd, but faded swiftly into silence, like water seeping into the sand.

"To the first accusation—namely, that I, Guin, am a demon come from the Land of the Dead to wreak vengeance upon the Lagon—this could not be more untrue. I cannot understand why you might think such a thing. I am no creature of death! As you can see, I live and I move. Red blood flows in my veins; I know thirst, I know hunger. I can speak your words, walk upon two legs, and fight with two arms. This is what it means to live.

"The dead are cold and lie beneath the ground without moving, and when by sorcery they do move, they need neither food nor drink. They do not raise swords to fight, but breathe foul vapors that bring disease, or turn their enemies to stone. Do I seem a demon to your eyes? Do I seem such an unholy creature? I eat, like you, and wield a blade to cut my foes. I do not use some demon-spell to rot their flesh.

"Yes, I came from the desert, but I was not born there, and it is not the Land of the Dead, as you say. You know the Sem, and other living things that thrive in those sands. The desert dunes are not entirely unlike your mountain home. How can you call it the Land—"

"Kah!" One of the Lagon stood. He was a young warrior, about the same height and build as Guin. He spoke with barely restrained excitement. "He claims the word of *lagon* is a lie! The desert is the Land of the Dead. Even a child of three knows the Sem and the yidoh, and the sandworms, are demons in a land of decay. He profanes Aqrra! Make your judgment, and have him hung on the end of a spear."

A great chorus of agreement rose up, yet Guin could hear there were some dissenters. Still, it was a failure. Without knowing it, he seemed to have stepped over the line and profaned a Lagon taboo.

"Wait!" he shouted above the rising swell of the crowd. "I have not finished my explanation! If the Lagon are fair and honor their laws, then you must not pass judgment before you hear all I have to say—is this not so, Kah the Wise?"

"The Warrior with the Head of a Beast is correct."

The six-fingered sage lifted his malformed hand slowly, speaking in a steady voice. "Continue your explanation. Ran, you will hold your tongue until he is finished."

Guin bowed to the sage in thanks. Then he continued, testing each word gingerly, as though stepping on thin ice across a rushing stream. "Yes, I came through the desert. Yet this was only because there was no other way to reach your village. I fought with many creatures in those sands. Isn't the fact that I passed through this 'Land of the Dead' and remained a living being proof that I am not a demon? You look at me, at my head, and call me a demon from the desert. Yet, just as I crossed through the sands but was not born there, so too I wear this head though I was not born with it. It was a curse that made me as I am today. Beneath this head of a beast…is a face like yours.

"Now, as for the other accusation—that I am a thief come to steal your salt. Never before have I visited your mountain home. I came to speak with you, and your wise leaders. Yet I did not know exactly where the Lagon village lay, nor did I know the ways of your people. I did not know the white salt was precious to you, nor did I know that placing it in my provision-bag was a sin, for no one had ever told me this. Had I known, I would never have done something so foolish as to profane that which is sacred to the Lagon. I explained this to the ones who seized me, and I gave them the salt I had put in my bag. You will know this is true if you speak to the warriors who captured me.

"I regret from my heart that I broke a taboo of the Lagon, and I offer my apology. Yet I did it without knowledge of my sin. If breaking a taboo in ignorance is still a crime, then punish me—yet should not the punishment be different from that reserved for a crime committed in full knowledge?

"Think of this, too: were I truly a demon, it would have been a simple matter for me to bewitch those who found me with a spell, and leave the valley with your salt in secret. Yet I did not do this, but instead threw down my weapon, returned the salt, and was brought to your village to be thrown into prison.

"I did not choose to fight with the Lagon, because I want to be your friend. I have come here, braving many hardships in my journey, to ask for your mighty aid.

"How will you Lagon treat me now, knowing the truth I have told you—can you be as fair as you claim? Will you kill me without considering what I have to say? I leave that to your sense of justice.

"This is my explanation. I offer it before you, Kah the Wise, and all the fair people of the Lagon."

Guin fell silent, and boldly looked around at the gathered

wildlings. The effect of his words on his audience was clear. Throughout the crowd Lagon turned to each other, gauging their companions' reactions, and began to whisper in hushed voices, seeking a unity of opinion. It appeared that Kah's silencing of the young warrior early on had quieted the younger generation, leaving this decision in the hands of the elders.

Kah the Wise said nothing. He merely stared at the leopard-man from under his bushy brows for so long that even Guin began to worry. In silence the ancient wildling clasped his hands—Guin now saw that they both bore six fingers—together upon his lap, and sat still.

Guin was about to ask if some decision had been made when Kah's voice cut him off. "Judgment will come after all has been heard. Now, Warrior with the Head of a Beast, let us hear how you intend to prove the most important words you have said: that you were sent here to lead the Lagon to the true path by Aqrra."

"Well..." Guin began, then stopped.

"Have you no answer?" Kah demanded. "You said you were a messenger from Aqrra. Then let me ask: What is Aqrra? What is Aqrra's form? Have you seen Aqrra? Show us proof you are a messenger."

"Proof, proof!" the crowd chorused behind him.

Guin felt cold sweat trickle down his back. He had not anticipated standing here under the pale wildland moon to be asked questions about the wildlings' religion. He searched his patchwork memory for anything that might help, but came up with nothing. Guin shook his head, unsure of how to reply.

"Aqrra is everywhere," he said at last, feeling much like a small craft setting out to sea in the middle of a storm. At the mercy of the waves, he would paddle for all he was worth. "Aqrra is known by many names. As the Lagon know him by one name, I know him by another. None can know where Aqrra resides, for he is everywhere, and nowhere. No man has met Aqrra, for no man may stand in his presence."

"Indeed," Kah the Wise replied, quite unexpectedly. "Continue."

"There are none who can describe Aqrra's form, for none are able to see him. Yet he exists above us all—he is the creator of all."

"Enough!"

Again, Dodok the Brave's voice boomed above the gathering. His tone bespoke terrific rage. The leopard-man fell silent immediately. He had tried to keep his descriptions so vague they couldn't possibly be faulted, but perhaps he had said too much.

Dodok the Brave rose to stand on the broad seat of his stone chair. The hard lines of his face shone wetly in the moonlight, his features twisted with fury.

"Enough! This beast-man is no messenger of Aqrra. He knows nothing of Aqrra at all. All his words are blasphemy, all that passes through his lips. Aqrra is not as he says. Aqrra can be seen with the eye. Aqrra is not everywhere and nowhere. Aqrra is where it is. Do we not say that if it is lost, the Lagon will be destroyed? He says Aqrra has a different name. But Aqrra is only Aqrra. Why? *Because none other than* lagon *know Aqrra.* The beast-head lies! He says the creatures of the outside world know Aqrra. He claims to have come on Aqrra's orders, to proclaim Aqrra's will. Yet he does not know Aqrra! I will not hear another of his lies! Kill him, kill him, kill him! Do any contest the judgment of Kah the Wise and Dodok the Brave?"

"None, none, none!" rose shouts from the crowd.

"Kah will give his blessings to Dodok!"

"Kill the beast-head!"

"Kill him!"

The shouts of the crowd echoed off the heights of the mountains around them, drowning out the far-off crying of the wolves.

"Kill him!" Dodok howled.

Guin's thoughts dissolved in bleak dismay. Apparently, this Aqrra was not a person, nor a god, but some sort of object. Something was tugging at the back of Guin's mind, but he didn't have time to pay it any attention.

"Kill, kill, kill, kill!"

"Kill the demon!"

All around the clearing, the hirsute giants stood and thrust clenched fists into the air. Guin knew the situation was grim, perhaps the worst he had ever faced. Yet, a thin shred of hope remained.

Kah had not yet added his voice to the cacophony. However, the wizened elder didn't seem particularly interested in stopping it, either. His eyes were closed to mere slits, and he sat with hands clenched, as though in a trance.

"Rip him apart! Rip him!"

The crowd was hungry for blood.

"Kill, kill, kill!"

No good, thought Guin, giving up on any hope of a rescue from Kah. It was beginning to look like his only way out might be to fight his way to freedom. He took stock of the crowd. To his dismay, the numbers had grown since he arrived. There might well be a thousand Lagon around him, each one of them near his height if not considerably larger.

Another strategy suggested itself. *If I can take Kah the Wise as a hostage...* Guin tensed every muscle, preparing to duck past the stone-tipped spears of the guards and charge the leaders' chairs.

"But he said he could defeat Dodok the Brave!" came a sharp high voice from the crowd.

"Rhana!" came the hushing of a parent. "Mind your tongue."

"But the leopard-head said he was strong!" the child Rhana went on, undaunted. "Stronger than Dodok the Brave. He said he came to show to everyone, he is the true Brave. Why do they not fight?"

A complete silence settled suddenly over the crowd, different from the one Kah the Wise had called for earlier. It was a silence rigid with fear, and apprehension.

"Rhana!" the Lagon that must have been Rhana's mother shouted in a horrified voice. Guin scanned the crowd, finally spotting his little friend standing amidst a group of Lagon to the left of Dodok. Her round eyes stared at Guin unblinking.

"He is short," she said. "How can he be stronger than Dodok? Why will Dodok not fight him?"

"It is because Dodok is afraid of me!" Guin declared, seizing the opportunity. "Lagon! Braves of Lagon! Dodok would kill me without a fair trial, without even a fair fight!"

"Silence, demon!" Dodok roared, leaping down from his chair with a spasm of rage. His face was flushed with fury. "Who is afraid of a runt such as you? The Lagon are fair! You are a demon! You were brought here to explain yourself, not to fight. The Lagon will not fight demons!"

"The Lagon will not fight, or Dodok will not fight?" Guin challenged. "The Lagon are a brave, true people. But their leader Dodok is a coward. He is afraid to fight me. Why? It is because he knows that if he fights me, he will no longer be the strongest!"

A communal gasp rose from the crowd. The air stank of fear and sweat.

Dodok took a slow step forward. He was no longer shouting, though the rage boiled behind his clenched teeth, a far more terrifying sight than his outburst a moment before. He loomed, nearly three *taal* high, looking down at the leopard-headed warrior before him.

"Now you would shame me, *lagon* with the head of a beast?" Dodok asked, his voice trembling with the eerie quiet that comes just before an explosion. "Shame me without a challenge, and I may kill you. Or adhere to the code, and challenge me, for the chance to prove your words are true."

It was an easy choice. "I challenge Dodok the Brave," Guin replied immediately. As one, the Lagon held their breath. Before them all, Guin had challenged Dodok the Brave, strongest of all the braves, twice as formidable as himself. Many shook their heads, assuming that, in his fear, their strange captive had gone mad. Guin continued. "However, I do not know the rules of combat among your people. I would have you teach me. I would challenge Dodok."

"Good!" Dodok howled. "I accept your challenge! On the honor of Dodok the Brave, I will rend you to pieces!"

Then abruptly he fell silent and turned to Kah the Wise, as though awaiting a final permission. Guin made note that of the two chiefs, the Wise stood above the Brave.

Kah the Wise was lost in thought behind half-lowered lids, yet after a moment he widened his eyes and spoke to the silent crowd.

"Very well. Our purpose here is changed. Dodok the Brave will fight the Warrior with the Head of a Beast. If Dodok wins, Guin shall die. Should Guin prevail, we will consider his claim to be true, that he is a messenger from Aqrra."

Guin was impressed. It was a keen political move. With those words, Kah the Wise had managed to ensure that even if Dodok should lose, the Lagon would lose nothing.

"Are there any objections?" Kah asked, slowly turning his head to scan the crowd. Dodok and Guin eyed each other silently.

All at once the angry energy of the Lagon rushed away like a tide, replaced by excitement for the spectacle that was to come. It was clear that the giant wildlings loved nothing more than watching a good fight, and tonight would be a show to remember.

"Prepare yourselves," Kah the Wise ordered. "This ground will know combat before the rising of the sun."

Dodok the Brave stretched to his full height and sauntered into the clearing, where he turned to look again at his challenger. His eyes were filled with anger and disdain, shot through with a cruel joy at the slaughter to come.

Guin wordlessly returned his gaze. At last—for the time being, at least—things were going as he had hoped. Now all he had to do was defeat Dodok and convince the Lagon to listen to him.

Above his head, the moon shone with a cold light, illuminating the stone buildings and the ample-haired creatures that filled the streets between them. Only three or four *twists* of the sand-clock remained until dawn.

4

"You are prepared?"

The low voice of Kah the Wise carried clearly across the silent amphitheater, drifting over the heads of the assembled crowd.

"Dodok is ready," the massive Lagon chieftain replied, nodding slowly.

"As am I," Guin asserted.

One thousand or more Lagon sat around the giants' gathering-place—warriors, women, children, elders—all with eyes fixed on the two combatants. It was well past midnight, yet even mothers clutching small infants to their breasts were present. The Lagon loved battle—so much that they used one-on-one combat to determine who led them—and even at this improbable hour, the eagerness of the spectators was palpable. No one wanted to miss the event.

In Middle Country terms Guin was a man of legendary

proportions. Yet to the mighty Lagon, who averaged two *taal* in height and one hundred *skones* in weight, the leopard-headed warrior appeared rather puny, standing eye to eye with young boys and the shorter womenfolk.

And if Guin was a runt among the Lagon, Dodok the Brave was a giant among giants. He stood like an animate mountain in the midst of the clearing, arms crossed upon his chest, waiting for Kah the Wise to give the signal to begin. Naked save for a loincloth of ragged hide, he stood a full *taal* taller and weighed half again as much as his challenger.

Though most of the Lagon were slender for their height, Dodok was proportioned much the same as Guin. The hair swirled down his back in a great mane, and bristled in clumps of yellow and brown on his stomach, chest, and arms, barely concealing the powerful sheets of muscle beneath.

Yet his sheer mass did not mean he lacked agility. Though tall, the Lagon were neither heavy-boned nor clumsy. Even those who towered over two *taal* moved swiftly, their reflexes honed over years of hunting wolves and lizards through the rocky hills they called home.

The gaze of the packed crowd flamed with hostility as it looked upon the intruder, the blasphemer, the upstart challenger Guin. Most did not watch to see whether Dodok or Guin would emerge victorious; rather, they waited breathlessly to see how Dodok the Brave, their indomitable chieftain, would take this brazen, foolish creature and toy with him, break him, and then rend him limb from limb. This was the source of the excitement that stirred the air with rank sweat and seething blood. Guin understood this well, perhaps better than any other. Yet his glinting yellow eyes and the leopard mask through which they shone revealed no trace of fear.

"To me, childling!" Dodok taunted, and his eyes said: *it is beneath me to make the first move.* Grinning with calm confidence, he lifted a terrifyingly large fist and pounded his rippling chest.

Guin kept his distance, his cool gaze marking their positions, his toes finding purchase in the light, rocky sand. It was apparently a custom of the Lagon to fight unarmed. Normally, this might ensure fair combat, yet in the current situation, it seemed a bad jest. Dodok's long arms, giant frame, and fearful strength were a far more lethal assortment of weapons than any set of blades would have been.

Despite Guin's own considerable strength, he knew that if the giant's hands should grab him, it would be no simple feat to break free. He could writhe and twist all he wanted, yet those powerful arms would drag him into a killing embrace, bending his neck back until it touched his spine.

There would be little chance of victory in close-quarters wrestling, Guin decided, his feet dancing across the sand as he dexterously began circling around his opponent's right side. He would wait for the Lagon's charge, duck aside, and attempt to leap on Dodok's back.

Dodok made a sound like a growling laugh from deep within his throat, and almost carelessly took a step forward. He moved with all the confidence of one who has read his enemy's thoughts and knows the outcome of the match before even the first blow has landed.

As Guin continued his move to the side, Dodok's long arm thrust out swiftly, blocking his path. Then the giant turned, hands apart, fingers hooked inward like claws, and slashed at the leopard-man's head.

Swiftly Guin pivoted and lunged back to the left.

Again, Dodok was there before he could slip past, and Guin was forced to retreat.

"What's wrong?" Dodok chided. "I thought you were stronger than Dodok! All you do is run. How will you prove your strength?"

A chorus of cheers rose up from the Lagon. Guin bared his fangs at them in reply. All the while, his feet kept up their dance, slowly shifting his position.

Finally, Dodok lost his patience. Done with caution, he lunged with both arms extended toward his diminutive prey. For all his bulk, the Lagon chief moved impossibly fast.

Guin jumped lightly backward. Dodok closed the distance. Guin darted to one side, but Dodok regained his balance too quickly, and Guin was unable to flank him and they were facing again. Dodok sneered and lunged again, but this time Guin thrust out his leg to trip him. It nearly worked, but after three unsteady steps, Dodok was balanced again, and Guin was forced to jump back, maintaining his calculated range.

"You intend to run until dawn, demon?" Dodok roared, his irritation unconcealed. He spread his long arms, inviting Guin to grapple with him. The leopard-headed warrior kept his distance.

By now the crowd had gone from making occasional catcalls to openly berating Guin, angry at the interloper's refusal to fight. Some whispered that this wasn't combat at all, but some sort of demon dance. Others wondered if Guin was trying to wear Dodok out—and shook their heads at the runt's foolishness.

When the leopard-man moved, he moved as fast as lightning. For a moment, it looked as if he were charging headlong into Dodok's embrace, yet at the last possible second he ducked beneath the Lagon's outstretched arms, going for his legs. The tactic worked. Guin hooked his left foot behind Dodok's right shin and swept out the giant's leg, sending his towering opponent heavily onto his back. By the time the cursing Lagon had regained his feet, Guin was already out of reach, across the clearing.

The Lagon chief stood, his face a red mask of rage. "Enough, demon!" he howled. Stretching out his arms to their full length once again, he charged with fearsome speed. Guin did not dodge this time. As Dodok's long arms came down to grab his shoulders, he hunched down low, using his body as a fulcrum to throw his opponent completely over him.

"Yarr!"

As one, the crowd gasped in surprise.

"He threw Dodok!"

"The little demon lifted him!"

Dodok did not fall gracefully. He slammed into hard, rocky ground headfirst, then toppled over onto his back. Staggering quickly back to his feet, he turned to fix Guin with a glare so filled with menace it would have frozen a lesser man cold in his tracks. Gone was the taunting, jeering Dodok of moments before. Now he stared with bloodshot eyes, insane in his rage. The war-chief of the Lagon was chosen by tournament; the moment his strength came into question was the moment he began to lose his mandate. The smaller Guin had now thrown him twice, making him crawl on the ground in front of the entire village. Even if he went on to rip Guin to pieces, this poor beginning meant that, over the next few days, he would surely have to face several more upstarts from the tribe to secure his standing.

Dodok roared with frustration. Yet the last toss had taught him caution. He gave up lunging with both hands, pausing instead to study Guin's every motion. The leopard-man let his arms hang at his sides in apparent carelessness, inviting an attack.

To each warrior, the other's position was clear: Guin, overpowered, needed to use his enemy's strength against him. Dodok needed to watch Guin closely to avoid losing his advantages to a well-timed feint.

The giant bared his teeth defiantly, clenching his fists and glowering at the leopard warrior. Slowly but surely, the massive Lagon began to close the distance with his prey.

Guin dodged to the side. Dodok followed. Guin circled to the left, and Dodok whirled to meet him; Guin shifted to the right, and Dodok was there. So the two combatants traded move and counter-move in a silent killing dance, their positions ever changing, neither gaining a clear advantage for long.

"Dodok! Dodok!" came impatient shouts from the bloodthirsty crowd. They couldn't understand why their towering chieftain didn't just pick up his tiny opponent and be done with it, and the wait was beginning to cool their excitement.

"Fight! Fight!"

"Grab him, Dodok!"

"Dawn is coming! Fight!"

"Dodok!"

Dodok stood impassively, seemingly heedless of the cheers and cries for blood. He was no fool, and he would not enter combat at a disadvantage just to please the eager throng. Hands crooked like claws, legs spaced apart, he circled around the center of the arena slowly, patiently.

This time, it was Guin's eyes that sparked with a faint color of irritation.

Again and again, Dodok the Brave warily closed the distance between them, then sprang suddenly forward; again and again, Guin leapt safely aside, and the circling resumed. It was just after one such maneuver that the leopard-man let his eyes wander for an instant, glancing up over the mountains that surrounded the village.

Above the stone chair placed among the row of spectators, where sat the white-haired, many-fingered Kah the Wise, his eyes half-lidded in seeming disinterest; above the stone steps circling the place of combat, filled with shouting warriors, cheering women, and sleepy-eyed children; above the soaring black silhouette of the mountains, jagged as a broken crown, there stretched the wide dreamlike sky, brilliant yet ephemeral in the delicate light of pre-dawn. It was a sight that no painter could have duplicated, not even in a lifetime of the highest skill. So divine was its hue, so filled with the limitless meaning and delicacy of which only nature was capable, that even in the midst of the battle a bolt of recognition flashed through Guin's brain.

As the two warriors fought, dawn was slipping out of the darkness.

The fire chariot of the sun god Ruah had not yet appeared in all its magnificence over the edge of the mountains. Nor were the clouds blushed with the first traces of pinkish light that heralded Ruah's coming. Yet, as sure as Aeris wheeled through the sky toward the horizon, the night was drawing to an end. Above the combatants and the spectators, all focused single-mindedly on the struggle playing out upon the patch of empty ground at the bottom of the town-basin, the air had begun to fill with an almost audible premonition of the day, and the sky was slowly shifting from indigo to blue.

It was the morning of the fourth day of Guin's quest—his last day. *His last chance.*

The leopard-headed warrior gritted his teeth to stem a rising tide of irritation and rage. For a fraction of a moment, his guard was down.

"Gwarh!"

Everything around him went black as Dodok's battle cry

rent through the half-lit quiet. Iron limbs, more powerful even than those of the grey ape of Gabul, seized the leopard-man's shoulders and drew him into a vise-like embrace.

Guin howled, twisting his body in a vain attempt to throw off that iron grip. His upper body blushed crimson, the muscles rising in taut bands over his shoulders, chest, neck, and arms.

Dodok let his full one-hundred-fifty *skones* of weight do the work for him. No matter how Guin struggled, the Lagon was irresistible. It was as though Guin grappled with a massive boulder, grown in the place of his flesh-and-bone adversary. All Dodok's strength went into his arms, slowly dragging Guin closer.

Then, inexplicably, the giant's grip loosened. Guin began to swing his arms upward to knock away the claw-like fingers digging into his shoulders—but he had fallen into a trap. The instant the leopard-man shifted his hands from their position braced against the Lagon's chest, Dodok brought his own hands down, pinning Guin's arms to his sides in a crushing bear hug.

A great cheer went up from the crowd. In one swift move, Dodok had made his victory almost certain. With a low growl he tightened his hold on Guin, squeezing until it seemed that his adversary's backbone would surely snap in half.

A beast-like roar escaped from Guin's mouth. He arched

his torso backward, scraping with his fingers at whatever he could reach. Yet still the grip tightened, threatening to fold him in two.

Dodok's eyes bulged widely, staring at Guin. The leopard warrior, his head cast backward, scrabbled with his fingers against his enemy, trying to dig into the iron muscles. For the first time, Dodok the Brave allowed himself a howl of victory.

The howl cut off halfway. Guin, his arms a deep purple from the strain, had worked his hands up Dodok's torso until he found the Lagon's arms. Now he grabbed those iron-like pincers and began pushing against the giant's grip.

Dodok's face went pale. For the briefest of moments—one that seemed to last for an eternity—the two became like statues, strength enough to crush rocks pushing inward against a similar strength pushing out. So evenly matched they were that, from a distance, they seemed poised in perfect calm. Only the hot sweat dripping from their faces and bodies revealed how desperately they fought their deadly contest.

The crowd was suddenly silent. Not a single cheer, or cry of "Dodok!" could be heard in the clearing. The mass of spectators held their breath, swallowed, and watched to see which way the scales would tip.

Suddenly, the balance broke. With a dull sound, Dodok's vice-like grip on Guin's body gave out.

Guin took his chance. Bending backward like a bow, he snapped his torso forward, slamming into his foe. Dodok spun once around like a top, and fell on his back, sprawling across the ground. Guin fell atop the giant. With the last of his strength, Guin slid out of Dodok's limp embrace and sprang away, only to fall to one knee, his back bent, exhausted.

For some time Dodok did not move. A murmur ran through the crowd. *Is he unconscious? Is he dead?* A breath that was part shock, part fear passed through the crowd. Just as quickly it became a cheer, as Dodok the Brave sat up.

A trickle of blood ran from the giant's mouth, and his left arm hung limp. Yet his eyes burned with unquenched rage: *You may fight me, but you will lose! I am Dodok. Dodok the Brave!*

Through a haze of pain, Guin saw his opponent charging, off kilter, his good right arm stretched out in front of him. There was no sound, no howl of rage. Dodok hurtled forward in utter silence. All hatred and derision were gone from his eyes. All that was left was his warrior spirit, stronger than any anger.

Guin stood to meet the charge. A bolt of pain jabbed down his spine, and he clenched his teeth to stifle a cry of pain. As he flexed his back he knew that he did not have strength enough remaining to finish this opponent, even injured as the Lagon was.

Surrender, however, was not an option. The warrior spirit that rose in Dodok's blood shone too in Guin's leopard-yellow eyes, blazing as he stared forward. Unthinkingly, he dropped to one knee again and groped at his belt—an unconscious, instinctive motion to seek something he could use as a weapon.

His fingers found something hard and cold. Instantly Guin whipped it out, though his blurry eyes had trouble focusing on it. He thrust the object at the careening Lagon chief in blind self-preservation. Blade or no blade, whatever the object was, he would make it hurt Dodok, or he would pay with his life.

But the charge never came. In the utter silence that had fallen, Guin forced his aching eyes to focus on the cold object in his hand.

The leopard-man had needed a miracle to win, and he had got one.

Chapter Two

Dawn Surprise

— I —

"Aaah!"

A great cry rose up—and then all sound ceased. Every giant in the amphitheater of the Lagon instantly grew still. It was as though all of them had been turned to stone, like the people of Kanan in the legend of the lost empire. The silence that gripped the mountain vale was filled with meaning, the premonition of a great change both subtle and complex.

All the Lagon, even Kah the Wise, held their breath, their voices robbed from them by what they saw. Their power to move, their ability to think—everything was paralyzed. Wide-eyed they huddled, a silent throng, a crowd of awestruck statues.

Around them the mountains towered, jagged crags looming high above the barren valley and its village of stone. Already, far beyond the dark slopes of the mountains, the pale white sphere of Aeris the moon goddess, ever shy, hurried to hide herself. The first rays of morning that heralded the arrival of Ruah's golden chariot would soon reach the valley floor.

The portent-filled predawn light bathed the giant Lagon of Nospherus as they sat unmoving. Among the crowd one of the stone chairs of the chieftains sat empty; in the other, Kah the Wise was poised, leaning far forward, his eyes wide in awe, his six-fingered hands gripping the arms of his chair, his long robe reaching to the ground.

Every giant's gaze was fixed on the center of the amphitheater, where the arena was cut like a bowl from the valley rock. There, Dodok the Brave stood ready to leap, his hand extended—yet his feet were planted firmly on the ground, motionless.

Just before him, half-risen from the ground, was Guin. The leopard-man extended his right hand directly toward his foe, gripping the object he had instinctively pulled from his belt like a ward to fend off demons. It was clear from the way every eye was drawn to the object in his hand that this was the source of the enchantment that held the village in thrall; yet Guin, who wielded it, understood what was happening the least. Even when his foe stopped short in his attack, and a silence like the death of all creation fell upon them, he had no comprehension of what had happened. Guin too was frozen in place, a statue, as though caught in the very ensorcelment he had wrought.

Even had he dared look at what he held, he would have been at a loss to remember whence it had come, or what it was. He did not look; instead, like the legendary Irana brandishing the Sword of Victory, he held it up to the Lagon brave. It was as though the slender, silvery object sent invisible rays of power streaming in all directions to envelop the entire world, transporting it to an eternal dimension where time, life, and death were no more than dreams.

Guin feared that if he so much as twitched, he would break the bizarre spell that had overtaken the valley, and the interrupted combat would reach its bloody conclusion.

Yet, in that stifling silence and stillness, time had not stopped its motion but flowed on soundlessly. Though none there had the presence of mind to notice it, a great sunrise was beginning in the east. As he did every morn, the sun god Ruah rose above the land, spread his shining hands, and thrust them into the valley.

The first beam of light to strike the valley floor was greeted with a new cry from the crowd, and at once, the spell was ended. Like sunlight melting dew, the surprise and fear that hung heavy in the air unraveled into a tremendous yell of exhilaration.

"Look! Look!" the Lagon began to shout, their individual cries blending together until the valley shuddered with the roar. In the very midst of it all, Guin rose to stand, legs apart, brandishing the object in his right hand on high. He looked and knew for the first time that the oddly shaped silvery rod he held was the object he had seen sparkle in the valley of salt and, without thinking, picked up and thrust into his belt. But perhaps it had not been Guin who picked up the rod at all, but the rod that used Guin to enact its will.

In a flash the leopard-man was enveloped in the radiance of the morning sun, and the light reflecting off the rod was so bright it became impossible to look at it directly.

"Ohhh!" came a low moan from the crowd. It was Kah the Wise. The ancient sage clutched the wooden armrests of his chair so tightly that it seemed he would snap them in two, and he leaned forward so far he was in danger of toppling to the ground. "Aqrra!"

That started it. Until now, the crowd was lost in awe and confusion—now they had a direction.

"Aqrra! It's Aqrra!"

"Aqrra!"

"He is Aqrra's messenger!"

"It is as the legend says!"

"The sign of Aqrra!"

"Aqrra!"

Soon, the cries of the Lagon swelled into a single great

chorus, chanting, "Aqrra! Aqrra!"

A moment later, the wildlings were leaping from their seats. As one the giants of Nospherus ran toward the leopard-headed, bare-chested warrior in the middle of the arena, racing to be the first to prostrate themselves before him.

It seemed as if lightning had stricken Dodok the Brave, so fast did he fall at Guin's feet, practically kissing the chalk-covered toes of the man he had tried to strike down in mortal combat only moments before.

The object in Guin's hand sparkled in the gradually waxing morning light, and then, as though by some magic, a high, clear sound like breaking crystal rang through the air.

"Aqrra!" Every Lagon, warriors, women, elders, even children dragged by their mothers' hands, reached out toward Guin, bowing to the ground before him as though smitten with awe.

Once again silence filled the arena, but its character was different from the frozen hush of a moment before. This was a warm stillness that held not fear, but endless hope. On the stone steps of the amphitheater, two powerful Lagon warriors joined arms beneath Kah the Wise and lifted him slowly from the stone chair. Guin gasped. The six-fingered elder's legs were withered beneath his long robes. He could not stand on his own.

In reverent silence, the two warriors carried Kah the Wise gently down the stairs. The crowd parted wordlessly before him. When he reached the bottom they carried him up to the leopard-headed warrior. Kah motioned to the warriors and they set him down upon the earth next to where Dodok the Brave still crouched.

A brilliant ray of light shot down into the valley, enveloping Guin in a radiant aura. The rod in his hand chimed like a bell made of the rarest silver. Kah looked up at him, his eyes filled with a deep surprise and joy.

"Messenger of Aqrra," the sage said in a faint voice.

"Messenger of Aqrra!" echoed the Lagon.

"The...tales were true. I live to see their truth. Of a long line of wise and unerring Kah, this Kah the Wise that is me, has met a messenger of Aqrra. I meet the one who will lead the Lagon to the promised land."

Kah closed his eyes. Glistening tears ran in two lines down his ancient cheeks. "Aqrra, I give thanks," he rasped. Next to him, Dodok the Brave kept his head pressed to the ground.

Guin stood in the midst of all the Lagon's adoration and fearful reverence, bathed in light, his leopard head seeming for all the world like destiny given physical form.

Kah the Wise stretched out a hand, palm-first, toward the sign Guin carried. "You are Aqrra's messenger." The old

wildling's voice, though low, carried clearly to every corner of the stone village. "*Lagon* will follow you. *Lagon* will go where you lead, fight your enemies, and befriend your friends. Even if a battle bears no hope or benefit, if you say 'fight,' *lagon* will fight until the last warrior has fallen dead upon the ground. Even if you lead us to a barren waste, a valley of death and miasma, we will not doubt that it is Aqrra's promised land. You were the one chosen as Aqrra's messenger, to carry Aqrra's sign, to speak with Aqrra's words. Warrior with the Head of a Beast, *lagon* will follow you."

"*Lagon* will follow!"

The crying erupted from the mouths of every Lagon there and echoed through the valley.

"*Lagon* will follow!"

"*Lagon*!"

Guin reached out and took the six-fingered hand of Kah the Wise into his own. Though it seemed he had outlasted his need for the silver rod—the sign of Aqrra—he kept it held high in his other hand, just in case. The leopard-man looked once at the crowd bowed before him. Then he spoke:

"Lagon of Nospherus! I am come to ask for your aid. I am come to ask you to join me in battle." Guin's clear voice rang through the amphitheater. "Beyond your valley, across the valley of salt, across several dunes and the wasteland plains, a great army has invaded this land of Nospherus from beyond the flow of the Kes. Even now, a great Mongauli host faces the unified tribes of the Sem. The Sem resist the Mongauli, but the Sem are far smaller and not as well armed—and yet, although they are at a disadvantage, they yield not one grain of sand without a struggle. The fighting has been bitter, but the Sem believe it is their divine duty as children of Nospherus to drive back the invaders. I am come to ask the Lagon to help the Sem army. You, too, are children of Nospherus, and you must defend your home from the warriors of Mongaul who come to usurp it for their own ends. Preserve it always as a free land for those who are born here to live!

"Time is short. The Mongauli army stands poised to deliver a final crushing blow to the Sem forces—and if the Mongauli should win, the Sem tribes will be annihilated down to the last woman and child, great corpse-fires will burn upon the sands, and soon the white valley you hold sacred will be overrun. For, once the Mongauli have destroyed the Sem, it is a certainty that they will next come to destroy the Lagon.

"I do not know what land Aqrra has promised to the Lagon, nor can I tell you why Aqrra has decided that the Lagon should join in this struggle. But what I can say beyond any doubt is that no matter where your promised land may lie, no matter what land it may be, in order to claim it you must fight. Lend your strength to defend Nospherus, and drive back the evil that threatens to consume it. I have come across valley and mountain to bring you battle, flames, death—and victory.

"Rise, Lagon. Rise, people of Nospherus! Hear my pleas and take up spear and axe! Even as we speak, men with no true claim to this land threaten to trample it beneath their horses' hooves!"

Even before the echoes of Guin's speech had died, the Lagon took up the cheer.

"*Lagon* will stand with Aqrra!"

"*Lagon* will follow Aqrra!"

"*Lagon* will fight!"

"Aqrra, Aqrra!"

Some among the giants raised swords of cut crystal into the air, or whirled stone axes above their heads, while others pounded their chests with their fists and roared. Women and children both clutched at their hair, howling praise for the messenger of Aqrra and the warriors of Lagon.

"Prepare! We prepare!"

"Make ready! Sharpen your axes! Fill the food-satchels!"

"War! We go to war!"

Their eager cries soon transformed into barked orders and excited conversation as with a single-minded purposefulness the wildlings went to prepare for battle.

"Be swift," Guin added. Then, seeing that his job was done, he lowered the curious artifact in his hand and thrust it once again through his belt. His eyes traveled across the rapidly dispersing crowd, then up toward the sky.

His request had ultimately met with success far beyond his hopes, but Guin was not the least bit happy. Inside that expressionless leopard head, his two bestial yellow eyes shone harshly, bright with an unbearable anguish. His big fists hung tensely by his side, twitching and clenching as though in seizure as he glared up at the great arc of the blue sky, rimmed by the rough-cut ridgeline of the mountains, and at the sun which now rose high into the morning.

A low growl spilled from his mouth.

The fourth morning comes. How can I move the Lagon across wolf-infested mountains and the endless desert to reach the Sem by nightfall? I cannot. They have no horses, and even with mounts, it would take two days to cross that distance. Nor can I rely again on such a miracle as the cyclone which carried me.

Guin wanted not four days, but fourteen—yet he knew the sandclock that hung over his head was not in the hands of the Sem, but the Mongauli army. Even four days was too long if the attack had already come.

All that was left to him was to reach the Sem as fast as he could. *When I arrive with the Lagon, let it not be to a barren field of corpses, a banquet for the mouths-of-the-desert. Let my Lagon army not fight a battle of mourning for the fallen Sem.*

Please, let me be in time. Time... Guin growled. *If I could, I would command time itself to stop.*

"Brave warrior Guin," came a deep, wild voice, jarring the leopard-man from his reverie. The massive form of Dodok the Brave loomed before him. "Brave Guin, I offer my apology."

From beneath Dodok's jutting brow, sharp-gleaming eyes peered downward, fixing on the leopard-headed warrior.

"Apology?"

"When I accepted your challenge, I did not know you were the true messenger. I should not have fought the messenger of Aqrra. It is not shameful to lose to the messenger, for he borrows Aqrra's strength, and Aqrra's strength is undying."

Guin stood silently, watching the towering warrior intently.

"I did not believe you spoke the truth. I give you my apology. Do you accept?"

"I do," Guin said, taking the Lagon's massive hand in his. Dodok seemed moved by the gesture, and bowed his huge head.

After a moment the Lagon spoke again. "Brave Guin, the enemies *lagon* are to fight—they are strong?"

"One against one, they would not be a challenge for even a child of the Lagon," Guin said with a laugh. "But they ride horses. And use weapons not of stone but of steel, and powerful bows. They wear not cured hides, but thick metal armor. And they are many—as many as five times the number of your warriors. What's more, they fight in groups. They will not fight honorably, one against one, as the Lagon do. Yet, most of them are shorter even than I, and they are not strong."

"Then they are weak. Weak, and many. Like ants facing the wolf." Dodok the Brave's hideous face twisted into a smile. His eyes shone bright as candles. "I will lead *lagon* to victory in Aqrra's battle," he declared, slamming his chest with a fist.

"I look forward to seeing your feats on the field of battle, Dodok the Brave," Guin said truthfully.

Dodok turned and began to walk away—then stopped abruptly and turned back to stare into Guin's eyes. "Brave warrior Guin. I...feel regret for fighting Aqrra's messenger, but..."

Guin raised an eyebrow.

"Guin. Brave Guin. I fight many battles, more than I count hairs on my body, but never lose to one smaller than Dodok. You are smaller than Dodok. But you are strong. Brave Guin, I..."

"I understand," Guin said. "I, too, regret that our combat had to end before a clear victory was decided. Once we have prevailed in this battle Aqrra demands of us, should you and I both stand unharmed upon this land, we will pick a day of good omen, and we will fight until a winner is decided. Yet I have many things to do, so we will not fight until one is dead. We will fight until one lies unconscious upon the ground. The one standing shall be the victor."

"Good," Dodok the Brave said, his face suddenly brightening. Grinning, he clapped Guin on the chest with his massive hand before running off to assist with the tribe's preparations for war.

All around the amphitheater, skins, stone axes, and spears were piled into great heaps, and a great number of Lagon were busy among them. Guin lifted his eyes and spotted a Lagon child standing a short distance away from the crowd. It was Rhana.

Guin beckoned her closer. At first the girl seemed hesitant, but when Guin softened his gaze and called to her, she meekly approached.

"Hello, Rhana," Guin said, gently extending his hand and patting her on the head. "Thank you. Because of your kindness, I ate and drank, and was able to fight Dodok the Brave. May you know happiness always. You saved my life."

"Is Guin stronger than Dodok?" Rhana asked, her hesitant shyness draining away the closer she came to Guin. Gradually she seemed more at ease until she stood before the warrior and allowed him to embrace her in his arms.

"That I do not know," Guin told her. "We have just promised each other to find out for certain someday. But not soon. Know this, though. Dodok is very, very strong!"

Rhana's round eyes looked up at Guin's leopard head. Gently, she raised a hand and stroked his fur. "Is this a skin you wear?" she asked with a child's curiosity.

"It is not. For reasons I do not understand, I cannot take it off."

"Will everyone go to fight with you? Even Dodok?"

"Yes, they will."

"Rhana will go too."

"Rhana can go when she is bigger."

Guin lifted the Lagon child in his arms. He held her close, feeling her warmth and innocence drain away some of the urgent haste he felt consuming him from inside. Even though she was a child, her size made her heavier than a full-grown woman of the Middle Country.

"Will you come back to the valley of the Lagon?" she asked.

Guin answered honestly. "I do not know. I do not know what will happen. What I do know is that things will go as they are meant to go."

Rhana furrowed her brow a moment, then she seemed to give up trying to understand. She smiled. "Was the salted meat to your liking?"

"Ah, it was delicious."

"You want more?"

"No, later," Guin said, patting Rhana on the head. Her hair was soft and smelled of the sun and chalk powder.

Rhana looked as though she were about to ask another question, when a voice interrupted her.

"Guin, messenger of Aqrra. Kah the Wise wishes words. Please come to his house." It was one of the two warriors he had seen carrying the elder before. Guin surmised that this man was probably bound to the elder, serving as both his feet and his mouth to deliver such messages.

"Very well," Guin replied, and followed after him, with Rhana still curled in the crook of one arm.

The house of Kah the Wise was near the top of the stone-built village. Though small, it was immediately recognizable, for it had been crafted with rocks of a reddish hue, perhaps to set it apart from the other dwellings nearby. Guin set Rhana down before the rough-cut door to the elder's house, and patted her one last time on the head.

The Lagon girl dashed away, frequently glancing back at Guin as she made her way down the village's sloping main pathway. He watched her leave, then turned and went into the home of Kah the Wise.

— 2 —

Guin found the inside of the simple house to be stark and gloomy, with a heavy chill in the air of the kind peculiar to stone buildings. In its construction, the building was hardly more advanced than the pit-dwellings of the Sem. There was only one room; the morning light spilled in through three windows cut into the walls, splashing across an earthen floor that was bare save for a scattering of wolf skins laid around the central fire pit.

The elder had been placed upon one of the skins by the pit, and his keen piercing eyes now greeted the leopard-headed warrior. Kah motioned for Guin to join him, waved off the two guards, and began to speak before they had left the room.

"Brave Guin, as you have commanded, *lagon* now rise together. We leave our village, and head towards the land to which you lead us. There we will destroy your enemies. Whether it is victory or defeat that awaits us, this is the last morning we shall ever see this valley."

"I do not—" Guin began, but Kah lifted a six-fingered hand for silence.

"This is not unusual for *lagon*. *Lagon* are not bound to one place. Until we find the promised land, any place we live, we live only for the now, not for the ever. Aqrra sends us messengers, once every two or three generations. The last came when I was but a child. One of our people went out into the desert, and returned bearing the sign. Then a great journey began, and in the end we arrived here, in this place between the mountains, where we built this village of stone. *Lagon* do this. We will leave this village after this morning, and travel far to the place where the bearer of the sign leads, and there we will begin a new home. Should it be a desert, we will live in the desert. Should it be rock, we will live in the rock. Should it be a mountain, we will live on the mountain."

"I see," Guin said, nodding. "This must be why no one knows where the Lagon live—like running water, and as the legends say, you're never long in one place."

"It is so. Aqrra has shown us many lands, but none yet has been the promised land. Though we may think so at first, in time something comes to tell us of our error, and only then do we know that the latest sign from Aqrra was merely another portion of our journey, and that though we have not reached the promised land, we have taken a step closer to it. And so we live in our new home until the next sign comes."

Guin sat in silence, watching the old Lagon's eyes turn expressive beneath his bushy white brows. Something about the lives of these strange beings, following signs from their god, knowing that each might not be the true sign, again and again abandoning the homes where they had lived for some generations, touched him deeply.

"We are the ones who wait," Kah went on quietly. "This is what *lagon* means. Since time immemorial we have believed it is our destiny to wait, our destiny to follow. Yet, if that destiny is at its end with this new sign... How long we have waited! How often fought amongst ourselves, torn between those who would follow the sign, and those unwilling to abandon the land they had worked for since they were born... If—if you are indeed the last, the one who will lead *lagon* to the promised land..."

Kah's voice trailed off into overwhelmed silence. He lowered his head, intertwining his twelve fingers, at a loss for words to describe what it would mean for his people if Guin were the final messenger.

A thought twisted suddenly in Guin's mind, and he trembled. What if he was wrong? What if he was persuading the Lagon to abandon their village and travel far across the desert for nothing—to go to their own deaths as likely as not, in a battle that was not their own? For a moment, he doubted his right to move an entire people like this. The Lagon believed he was the long-awaited messenger chosen by Aqrra. But Guin had no idea whether he had indeed been so chosen.

The "sign of Aqrra" that he bore was little more than a strange object he had stumbled across in the valley of salt. True, he might have found it because some divine force intended that he should. Or he might be nothing more than a giant fraud. If it came to pass that both the Sem and the Lagon were defeated in this struggle with the Mongauli army, and their people slaughtered, he would be no god leading them to a promised land, but indeed a demon, a minion of Doal leading them to death, and despair, and destruction.

"How can you know the messenger of Aqrra, wise Kah?" Guin asked, doubts racing through his mind.

Kah's answer came simply and without hesitation. "He carries the sign of Aqrra."

"Like this thing I have?"

"Yes. Sometimes its appearance is slightly different, yet all resemble the one you bear."

"And how do the messengers come by their signs? Is it by some revelation from Aqrra?" Guin found himself asking the sage. Though he half-feared revealing too much of his ignorance about Aqrra and dashing the trust he had only so recently gained, he was unable to contain his curiosity.

He could not have been more surprised by the elder's answer.

"They obtain it as you did. A glimmer catches their eyes as they walk through the desert; they fall, they reach, and when they rise it is in their hands."

"What?" Guin exclaimed. "You mean they just pick it up?"

"Indeed. The finding of Aqrra's sign is a revelation nonetheless. Was this not the way you came upon the sign you bear?"

"That's just how it happened," Guin dropped his pretense. "To be honest, I know nothing of Aqrra—had not even heard of Aqrra before coming here. For such a person as I to have a revelation from Aqrra, to become a messenger... Can one be such a thing without knowing it?"

"Of course," Kah answered. "Yet what has made me think that you may be the true messenger, the last to lead the *lagon*, is that of the many times those claiming to be messengers of Aqrra have appeared before us—many of whom were little more than pretenders and would-be kings—in all the long years of the *lagon*, this is the first time that the one who has come is not one of us. Not only are you not *lagon*, but your leopard head marks you as one not of this world. It is the first I have ever heard of such a thing."

Guin made no reply, instead sinking deep into thought.

The familiar questions resurfaced in his mind: *Who am I? Whence did I come, and why? For what purpose was I given life?*

The questions hit him with such force that he forgot even the urgency that gnawed within him over the need to expedite the Lagon's march. *So many questions...* Even if he were to disregard his unknown origins, the leopard-man found himself surrounded by far too much mystery to be easily explained. What was the source of the bizarre knowledge that came to him in shreds, like scraps doled out to a dog by a master's hand—*whose hand?* He spoke the tongue of the Lagon, the tongue of the Sem, even the language of the Middle Country, yet he could not for his life tell which was his mother tongue. And the things he knew about the Middle Country—sometimes his memory seemed so clear, even though, to the best of his knowledge, he had never even been there.

The mystery did not end with what he carried inside him. He seemed to be involved in more inexplicable events than he cared to remember. How to explain the cyclone that carried him all the way to the Dog's Head, or his encounter with the ancient king of the wolves there—not to mention his finding and picking up the sign of Aqrra, placing it in his belt without a second thought, and drawing it out at just the moment that could save him? It was all too much coincidence for him to accept—indeed, no erudite man would be likely to believe it had happened at all. Yet it had.

And though his form, his great leopard head, made him an object of fear and mistrust among those he met, who frequently regarded him as a monstrosity, it seemed to him somehow right that he should wear it—as though he were merely following the orders of some greater power, moving according to the will of something so vast that no man could truly know it. Contemplating this possibility, Guin trembled.

If his speculations were correct, then he was no man possessed of a free will and moving according to his own wishes. Though he might feel that he was free, he was in fact little more than an oversized puppet, manipulated from the sky, or perhaps from below the earth—a marionette chosen to complete his stated task and no more.

He knew he should not dwell on such matters, yet it was impossible to stop. If it were true, and he was nothing more than a finger upon the hand of fate, he had no guarantee that whatever controlled him was not evil. What if that giant entity pushing him along through the world was not Janos or Jarn, the ancient wielder of fate's skein, but a servant of Doal, source of evils, or perhaps even Doal himself?

A shiver ran unbidden down Guin's spine. Kah the Wise turned a knowing gaze in his direction, marking how the warrior's neck tensed and trembled.

"As we use tools, so does fate use us," the ancient wilding said comfortingly. "Even if the revelation of Aqrra you have brought to us leads us not down the good path, but the bad, and even if many of us fall in the battle you have commanded of us, we will not call you a false messenger. It is vital that we follow the word of Aqrra, no matter what the consequences; for the consequences do not matter. What matters is that we are led by Aqrra, and follow Aqrra's word. Doing so is the reason our people exist."

Kah's simple words were filled with the highest kind of faith, and they surprised Guin greatly. "What is this Aqrra that holds so much power over your people?" he asked, his voice barely more than a whimper. "Is it a god? Or a man? Or something that has never been in this world? Tell me, why do the Lagon follow the lead of Aqrra so faithfully, without question?"

"Soon preparations will be complete, and we will be ready to leave this village," Kah said evasively, his mouth slowly curving into a smile. "Brave Guin, I see you are troubled, and have been for some time. I wonder, what is it that worries you? Have you made some promise that wears at your heart? Even when it was decided that we would join you, I saw not a moment's break from this trouble in your eyes."

"In truth, I am afraid I've run out of time," Guin told him, the admission made easier by Kah's keen perception. "To my allies I swore that I would return with the Lagon by sunfall tonight. When that time is up, there will not only be great danger to me; the twins of Parros, the little prince and princess who accompanied me across the desert, will be killed. Yet the sun is already in the sky, and we are far beyond the Dog's Head, and there is no way, save magic, by which I might hope to bring your warriors to the field of battle by nightfall today—for it is a distance that would take a horse two days to cross."

As he spoke, Guin felt the unease clutch at his chest with renewed vigor, and he thrust back his head and growled toward the sky.

For a while, the elder said nothing. He seemed to be deep in thought, but at last he nodded slowly, and opened his eyes. "If that is the case," he said, his voice as solemn as though he were uttering a sacred oath, "then we must make haste. Brave Guin—*lagon* are no common people. Many are the wonders that befall us. The revelations of Aqrra are but one of these. Deep, too, is our knowledge of this land of Nospherus, more than all other peoples combined. We may make the journey in time, or we may not. That is for Aqrra to decide. Brave Guin, later you must come to me and you must tell me of this place you wish to take us, you must describe it as best you can."

"I shall. But, if you do not intend some great sorcery, this place to which I take you now is a journey of ten days distant, perhaps more. It will take a full day merely to cross the Dog's Head." Guin frowned grimly. "Oh, but the Lady of Mongauli is right..." he muttered fiercely. "She chases after the Pearls of Parros unceasingly, and if her warriors cannot claim the secret of transport the twins hold, they will kill them—innocent children!—so that no one else might claim it in her stead.

"The secret the twins hold is too great, impossibly great—so powerful it could carry them from the burning Crystal Palace all the way to the Roodwood in the blink of an eye. How many generals, how many kings, would not sell their soul one thousand times over for the chance to wield such power..."

By the time he finished speaking, Guin's words had fallen to the faintest of whispers.

Kah the Wise looked on in silence. When he spoke, it was not in answer to Guin. "We will do what we can, and only Aqrra knows if we shall succeed or we shall fail. Yet I see you are still troubled, so to ease your worries I will talk to you of *lagon* until the tribe's preparations to leave are complete."

"I would like that very much," Guin said gladly. His curiosity had been piqued by the earlier conversation, and in any case he could do little until the Lagon were ready to depart. It seemed best to sate his curiosity; perhaps the elder's words would distract him from his worries.

"Aqrra...Aqrra is not a god," Kah the Wise began slowly. "Nor is Aqrra a living being. Aqrra—that which we call Aqrra—is a place."

"A place?" Guin said, gasping with surprise. "How can a mere place lead you, let alone show revelations?"

"It can," Kah said simply, his voice filled with iron faith. "This is because Aqrra is unlike any other place. Even as you said when you spoke before the *lagon*, it is a place where none may tread. If anyone were to face Aqrra, he would die standing. There are stories of those who have glimpsed Aqrra from afar, and according to these stories, around Aqrra, all is covered with the white bones of man and beast. Step upon them, and the bones shatter; a man's foot would sink deep into that white valley of death. This is the strange power of Aqrra. Yet as to what it truly is, none can say, for none can step near it.

"Yet each of those fallen bones, every single one, lies in line, pointing toward the center, and whether the morning sun shines upon it or not, Aqrra glows with a strange silvery light, and sometimes eerie voices and sounds not of this world can be heard there.

"Since the very first Kah the Wise of *lagon*, there have been many hundreds of Kahs, and all of them tell one tale. In this tale, it is said that it was Aqrra who made *lagon*. Aqrra fell from the sky with a blazing white light on a night as dark as death, and brought fiery ruin to Nospherus. Aqrra's strength was great, and none could escape it.

"Before the coming of Aqrra, *lagon* and *sem* were as one, neither larger nor smaller than the other. Yet when Aqrra descended, the chiefs of our two peoples were destroyed, and when they once again reappeared, they were *lagon* and *sem* as we know them today. You see, it was Aqrra who made us, and so *lagon* serve Aqrra and follow Aqrra's commands, for we were brought out of death by Aqrra.

"It is also said that Aqrra will one day rage again. When this happens, we *lagon* will stand and greet Aqrra, and by Aqrra's tremendous strength, all peoples in all lands but *lagon* will be turned to white bone. Only *lagon*, who serve Aqrra, will be forgiven this punishment and saved from the great miasma Aqrra brings."

Guin breathed deeply. The story was done. It was a strange tale, yet it did not sound like the empty rambling of some wildling fable-teller. Had Guin been at the Lady of Mongaul's war-pavilion, had he heard there the story of Cal Moru, magus of Kitai, who had crossed Nospherus by foot—the very story that had inspired the Mongauli invasion—he would have been deeply surprised, and alarmed.

Yet Cal Moru's tale was unknown to him, and he could not divine with any certainty which parts of Kah's story might be baseless legend, and which parts were a representation, however symbolic, of actual events.

"That is an amazing tale. However—"

Guin had just begun when two Lagon warriors rushed in through the rough-hewn doorway. They were dressed in full battle garb, and they bowed deeply to Guin and Kah before announcing that all the Lagon's preparations were complete. Then, linking their hands, they picked up Kah the Wise, and began to leave.

"Let us go. We must hurry, now," Kah said with a wave of his hand. He seemed to have entirely forgotten their conversation of a moment before. "We make for the Wind Hole."

"The Wind Hole?" Guin asked, but the wildling elder was already on his way out the door.

As Guin hurried out after him, he realized that he knew what it was that had been nagging at him since hearing the elder's story.

Aqrra... Why did it sound so familiar?

Was it not strangely similar to that word—Aurra—that Guin clung to as a token from his life before he woke beside the Roodspring?

It was yet another enigmatic coincidence.

—— 3 ——

The army of Mongaul was in mourning. The proud banners displayed at the head of the host now trailed sadly at half-mast, and the captains wore bands of black cloth bound about their arms and helmets—an unprecedented sight in the midst of such a fierce campaign. In ordinary times the stalwart warriors of Gohra would show no sign of grieving, even over close comrades, over brothers. There would be time enough for sorrow when the campaign was done. Until then the corpses could be left to rot upon the field.

But this time was different. The army which had borne the deaths of thousands grieved now for the loss of a single noble captain. Even the cruel death of Viscount Leegan had not slowed the Mongauli advance, but now the mighty invasion force had been staggered by the loss of Count Marus, leader of two thousand blue knights and lord of Tauride Castle.

On such a day of loss, the burden of command descended

with fearsome weight upon Lady Amnelis, the eighteen-year-old general of the Mongauli army. The certain knowledge that every soldier had pledged total loyalty to her—that these thousands of trained warriors functioned as an extension of her will and would unquestioningly lay down life and limb to carry out her commands—brought little comfort from the onus of her duty. The commanders of the army waited in uncertainty for Amnelis to decide on their next course of action. Even the faithful Astrias, whose admiration for the young general reached far beyond the bounds of mere loyalty, would have hesitated to say that the icy noblewoman was thoughtful or prudent. Amnelis was ice, but she was hot and passionate ice. When she was angry, her anger was fierce and direct—sometimes impetuous. The elder Marus, experienced and famous, had served to counterbalance the general's fierce intensity. Marus had followed Amnelis like her own shadow, his steady presence inspiring the soldiers to greater effort, reassuring their belief in their eventual victory. When the young lady made her decisions too quickly, the elder noble had restrained her, and when her wrath had fallen too severely upon her subordinates he had comforted the disheartened.

But now Count Marus was gone, and the Mongauli army wore its unheard-of symbols of mourning. A wordless quiet had settled on the army. The lady and her staff were the most silent of all: ever since Amnelis had received the sad news of Marus's death she had been inconsolable, weeping for the death of her "uncle" who had cared for her when she was a child. She seemed to have lost her fiery vitality; trusted officers who had once been close to her could no longer find ways to comfort her, and a pall of worry had settled over the army's high command. The leading knights could only observe now from a distance. They moved warily about Amnelis's tent, careful to make no sound.

Only Feldrik, Gajus, and some guards and servants had been allowed into Amnelis's pavilion, where the broad flaps of the entryway had remained firmly fastened since the tragedy. The sense of desperate uncertainty was almost more than the footmen and knights could bear. The Mongauli rank and file were as shocked by the death of Count Marus as their leaders, for his death had cast a grim shadow across all their future prospects. Uneasy murmurs rippled through their numbers.

"What will become of Mongaul?"

"Can the expedition continue without Count Marus?"

"How long are we going to carry on like this? When will we be allowed to go home?"

"First we lost Leegan Corps, and now all of Marus's blue knights. How can we call ourselves conquerors when Sem ambushes are cutting us down so fast?"

The battered army had dug in to lick its wounds at its latest bleak encampment. Intermittently the captains led their men through familiar drills while the restive horses stamped at their pickets. In their free time the soldiers sat around, sneaking smokes or nibbling dispiritedly at their scant provisions, quietly passing gossip. Ordinarily such behavior would never have been tolerated, but now even the troop captains seemed to have been infected by the low spirits of the camp, here upbraiding their aides over imagined faults, there resting beside their mounts with uncharacteristic lethargy, chewing vasya fruits and brooding silently. As often as not it was the camp orderlies who added to the confusion by spreading rumors from half-heard conversations. The rumors grew quickly as the anxious Mongauli could not but whisper amongst themselves. For all the soldiers' anxiety they had little choice but to wait—and brood—since Lady Amnelis remained secreted in her tent, not issuing orders, not even talking to her commanders. Gone was the stabilizing influence of the veteran Count Marus, who had shown equal skill at advising the lady-general and calming disturbances among the rank and file. Now the Mongauli began to feel that they had been led astray only to wind up stuck in a forsaken desert; the troops felt exposed and unprepared, surrounded by an ever-changing swarm of half-imagined perils.

In addition to the general disquiet, a certain particularly disturbing rumor, repeated uneasily by the soldiers, had begun making the rounds of the camp.

"Have you heard what they're saying?"

"About what?"

"You haven't heard, then? I can't believe it. It's about what happened to Count Marus! I got this from Yuvan, so I'm not sure if it's true or just another of his tales, but still..."

"Sure, sure! Just tell me what you heard!"

"Well, the long and short of it is, the reason Marus Corps got wiped out completely, is..."

"Yes?"

"Everybody is saying there was a traitor in their midst!"

"A traitor? Doalspit! I don't believe it!"

"Quiet! Not so loud!"

"But do you realize what you're saying? That one of our own brothers betrayed us?"

"I told you, not so loud! It's just a rumor...a rumor. Still, it makes sense. If someone in our army was trading secret messages with the Sem, he could easily have led Count Marus and his men into that hellish valley, and set 'em up for the ambush."

"But we are the proud knights of Mongaul! What kind of madman would debase himself by betraying us to those ignorant monkeys? Anyway, it's impossible. No one can speak their language, if you call that gabble a language."

"Like I said, it might be just a rumor."

At that point a sly-looking knight who was passing by stopped and joined the conversation.

"No, it's more than a rumor all right."

"Ah! Garum, you of the sharp ears! Have you heard something new? If you have, tell us!"

Garum drew closer and lowered his voice conspiratorially. "I'll tell you something I heard in secret from a friend in Irrim Corps. As you know, he led the soldiers who went to rescue Marus."

"Yes, yes..." The others gathered around the newcomer.

"There's no doubt that there was a spy."

"A spy?"

"I can't believe it!"

"It's true nonetheless. And by now our leaders know the name of this traitor even though they haven't told us knights. According to my friend in Irrim Corps, by the time the footmen entered the valley, most of Count Marus's knights had succumbed to fire and to the boulders and poisoned arrows the Sem had rained down on them. But not everyone died immediately. Irrim's men were moved to tears by the slaughter, but they still managed to beat down the flames. They found several survivors, terribly burned, who had kept alive by sheltering under the bodies of their comrades. These men were brought to Captain Irrim, and as they died they clutched at him with their peeling hands, and with what was left of their lips they whispered the story of their downfall—and the name of the traitor, the sole survivor, who escaped to continue his unclean alliance with the Sem."

"Great Janos! What are we going to do?!"

The knights glanced fearfully at the sky, as if it might suddenly collapse, and then regarded each other unhappily.

"Betrayed to the Sem. I still can't believe it!"

"Maybe my friend was just being stubborn, but that was his story; he insisted it was true."

"But how can humans and monkeys even make an alliance? Those Sem are nothing but filthy *monkeys*!"

"Yes—but they must be clever monkeys, to fight us as they have and lay a trap that tricked Count Marus!" Garum was annoyed that the others still doubted him. "Have you forgotten that monster that leads them? He's human, even if he wears the head of a leopard. Maybe he's the one who made a deal with our betrayer—not that he seems to need any assistance."

"But we didn't even see the leopard-headed warrior at the last battle..."

"Shoo," the others raised their voices to silence the

speaker, almost panicked by the mention of Guin.

"Don't even speak of him! That is an evil spirit hiding in the body of a man."

"Yeah, what if we called it to us, by speaking of it?"

The knight who had been hushed blustered, "Hah! I am not afraid of the monster. I hope I get the chance to unmask its true features."

"So you say. But I suspect those boasts would turn to screams pretty quickly."

"What...!"

"Oh, stop it! Anyway, if our captains know the name of the traitor, they'll deal with him sure enough."

"I suppose."

"They know where he came from. Marus Corps. Not many of them left to choose from, eh?"

"If they do know who it is, I wouldn't want to be in his boots when they catch him! Can you imagine what kind of torture he'll suffer when the Sem are defeated and we drag him in?"

"I still can't imagine why he would have done such a thing. Selling Marus Corps to the monkeys and the leopard-monster!"

"Aye... What was he thinking?"

"What kind of reward could he hope for in return for such treachery?"

"To become King of the Monkeys and to rule the yidoh and the wastes of Nospherus? 'Lord of All Nospherus,' surrounded by sand leeches and vampire moss, never able to see his friends or set foot in his home town again!"

"Hardly seems worth it, eh? Why, indeed?"

As the day dragged on the conversation continued haphazardly, the knights repeating the same questions again and again but finding no answers that they could believe.

"Treachery—but why? What was the motive?"

The same doubts dripped acidly from the lips of the Mongauli leader.

Amnelis had remained secreted in her pavilion for almost half a day, lost in the sorrow of Marus's death, with Gajus and Feldrik her only companions. During that time, Irrim of Talos Keep and his lieutenant Goran had been kept waiting outside, their requests for entry rejected by Amnelis's guards and servants until the two knights were nearly frantic. Although they, too, were saddened by the death of Count Marus, they were burning with the need to tell the Lady Amnelis what they had discovered; the long delay had strained the limits of etiquette. It was only after the two anxious warriors had stood for several twists sweating in the hot desert sun that they were finally permitted to enter.

The interior of the general's pavilion was swathed in gloom, the only illumination coming from a few oil lamps burning low along the walls. In the dimness Amnelis, wearing an informal bodice, reclined upon her divan; the shadows concealed the signs of recent grief on her face, helping to maintain the carefully cultivated image of strict composure of the Lady of Ice. But Irrim and Goran had no time for such details. As soon as they were admitted to her presence they began to spill out the alarming story of Marus's betrayal and the threat it posed to Mongauli unity.

At first Amnelis appeared to pay little heed to the dramatic tale, her face inscrutable in the shadows under the fall of her long blond hair. Gajus and Feldrik seemed to take more interest in the tale, but they held their peace while the black knights had their say. Finally, as Irrim stuttered on with excitement, his words tumbling out in disorderly bursts, Amnelis sat up on her cushions and stopped him short with her stinging voice.

"Treachery—but why? What was the motive?"

The lady-general's self-control had cracked; she uttered the two questions scathingly, fixing the two knights with a withering stare.

"It cannot be," she added. "What could any true Mongauli possibly want with the Sem? For what would he betray us?"

"Perhaps... Ah..." At a loss, Irrim and Goran looked at

each other and shrugged uncertainly.

Turning from them, Amnelis settled back into silent introspection. Then, abruptly, she stood and began to pace violently about the tent.

"I cannot imagine *how* it could have been done..." the lady spoke stiffly, twisting her slender fingers in agitation. "I just cannot believe it! None of my soldiers would even have had the opportunity to contact the Sem in secret during our endless battles across Nospherus. And what could the traitor gain by doing such a thing? What could the wildlings promise him? The chance to spend the rest of his life among the Sem, in the midst of desert monsters? What could half-witted monkeys possibly offer to make a Mongauli turn traitor? No, I cannot believe it."

"If..."

Everyone turned in surprise as Gajus broke his silence.

"If this person is indeed Mongauli."

Amnelis spun around quickly and glared at the runecaster. "What are you implying, Gajus?"

"Perhaps, my lady, we should consider the possibility that the traitor never swore loyalty to Mongaul in the first place. Perhaps he was an agent sent by fallen Parros, or by an enemy in Gohra—Kumn or Yulania..."

"Wait."

Amnelis ceased her pacing. She looked now as though she had recovered from her earlier shock. With a clap of her hands and a few quick gestures she summoned her servants and sent them to fetch cold drinks; then she turned again to her counselors.

"This is a serious matter, Gajus."

"Yes..."

"You realize that if what you just said is true, then the worst has happened. Our expedition is Mongaul's secret of secrets—if it stands revealed, we will never be able to recover. If indeed a traitor from outside Mongaul has penetrated our ranks disguised as a loyal retainer and has been privy to our plans, then the worst is true. That would mean the enemy's hand has reached the Marches patrol—and perhaps even into the Golden Scorpion Palace itself."

"I hesitate to ask if there is something you have, ah, overlooked..." Gajus directed Amnelis's thoughts obsequiously. "The twins of Parros, my lady. After they managed to escape from the Crystal Palace, despite all our efforts to apprehend them they managed to cross the River Kes and join the Sem in Nospherus."

"Ah!" Amnelis let out a low exclamation. Then she cried out again, louder, and struck her hands together furiously. "I *had* forgotten the Pearls of Parros! Somehow they slipped from my memory. What have I done!"

The lady seized a glass of honey wine from a servant and drained it in a single gulp, as if trying to calm her excoriated nerves. Then she commenced to pace about the tent again. But there was a difference in her movements, now—a fierce purpose—and it was obvious that beneath her blond hair her mind was working furiously. The rest of the company held their silence as she paced, and Irrim and Feldrik dropped their eyes to the floor, reluctant to intrude upon her thinking.

"Parros," Amnelis whispered, and then she raised her voice as though convinced. "Parros! That is it. I am certain of it now. Always it is Parros—every time! That old ensorcelled kingdom ever bars the way for Mongaul, vexing our ambitions! And now, unknowingly, we have let a spy of Parros among us!" The lady-general gnawed her lip in frustration, remembering the twins she had momentarily held in her grasp, and their freakish demigod-protector. Not only them—she thought, too, of the citizens of the crystal city who had desperately resisted her conquest. "Gajus!"

"Yes, my lady?"

"What is your opinion?"

"It is likely that you are correct. Our spies in Kumn and Yulania would have told us if those archduchies had discovered Mongaul's intentions, so it seems unlikely that the traitor came from either of them. I suspect the remnants of Parros have indeed formed an alliance with the Sem, since the wildlings have given shelter to the twins."

"If that is true, then our situation is very grave." Amnelis's lips tightened. "Feldrik."

"Yes, my lady."

"As soon as possible you must provide me with a list naming every soldier in this expedition whose history and identity is unclear."

"Certainly, my lady."

"If only we had realized this earlier—but no! Let us not think of that. If there are still some of Parros's agents among us, we must see to it that they do us no more harm." She paused, and the gleam in her eye grew colder before she spoke again. "Anyone of doubtful loyalty must not be left alive. Soldiers with unfamiliar accents. Those with relatives in Parros. Those with peculiar habits or questionable attitudes. Don't overlook anybody suspicious. Find them all and put them to the question!"

"Yes, my lady, I understand."

"Send out a command to the captains to make a note of any whom the Sem seem to have avoided shooting with their poisoned arrows or attacking during battle—and Irrim!"

"Yes, my lady?"

"The traitor's name—you said that a blue knight spoke the

name as he lay dying."

"Yes, my lady. Only one of the blue knights remained alive when we reached the valley, but he named the traitor—a man who had earned Count Marus's trust yet betrayed his debt of gratitude, a man who lied to the blue knights and led them into a trap in the village of the Sem, then sacrificed them to our enemies! It was said that Count Marus was able to hurl his sword and wound his betrayer in the right ear before the man fled."

"What is his name?" The Lady of Ice had regained her perfect self-control; her voice was firm and deliberate, although her knuckles whitened as she grasped a silver goblet.

Irrim lifted his bearded face and spoke clearly, his words seeming to resonate in the tent. "Eru of Argon."

"Eru of Argon..." Twice, three times Amnelis repeated the name, as if tasting an echo. Then she said coolly, "If this man should ever be captured by the knights of Mongaul..." The lady waved her hand dismissively, as if consigning the wretch to a fate so miserable it could only be guessed at.

"Yes, my lady, I understand."

Now Amnelis spoke slowly as though she had reached a final decision. "Feldrik, gather the captains at my pavilion. From this moment onward, we will permit no further arrogance from the Sem! Separate our scouts into small troops, and send them east, west, south, north—have them scour the desert until they discover the wildlings' main encampment! Until then the main body of the army will assemble here and prepare for the final decisive battle. You are not to let a single Sem, warrior, woman, or child, live to see tomorrow's sun. Is that clear?"

Feldrik bowed with deep respect. "Yes, my lady."

Amnelis's calm, quiet words had produced a greater effect on her subordinates than any yelling or display of temper could have. Feldrik had turned to hurry from the tent when the general's voice halted him.

"Additionally, tell the captains the name of Eru of Argon. Tell them that the one who catches him alive will receive a reward of ten thousand raan and a promotion in rank. If any should kill this Eru by mistake before he can be punished, that man will receive a hundred lashes before my eyes. I want the leopard-man, the twins of Parros, and the traitor taken alive. Don't leave any Sem breathing. Make sure the next battle will truly be the final one! No longer will I tolerate the wildlings' existence. If they retreat, drive them into a corner and slay them, and if they surrender, slaughter them where they stand. Is that clear? This will be Marus's funereal battle."

"Yes, my lady."

"Now go."

"Yes. My lady."

— 4 —

It was the morning of the third day since Guin had ridden forth to seek the Lagon. The combined force of the Sem, after two days on the move, was now resting at an oasis to the south of Dog's Head Mountain. After the most recent battle with the Mongauli army, the Karoi tribe had joined with the rest of the wildlings, and now their united army numbered nearly seven thousand. The Sem knew all of the oases in the vast Nospherus desert, and because of their numbers they had chosen to make camp beside the largest of them all.

Rinda and Remus were traveling with Loto's personal guard, accompanied by Suni and the Raku women. The twins were doing their best to put a brave face on their unease, but they had grown steadily more anxious since Guin had left them on his quest for reinforcements. Since they had first met him, the leopard-man had been their strength, their great protector. Although Suni and Loto treated them with kindness, the

Sem were savages nonetheless, and the twins were often frustrated by the fact that they could barely communicate with the wildlings who watched over them. Brother and sister often found themselves thinking back apprehensively over the events of the past few days.

The day after Guin departed for the east, the Sem army headed southward. Soon the main body of the wildlings joined up with the warlike Karoi, who were still in high spirits after their annihilation of Count Marus and his blue knights. Along with the welcome news of the victory, Rinda and Remus had found another surprise awaiting them amongst the Karoi—a familiar figure of human stature standing among the diminutive monkey-folk.

"Istavan!" The twins forgot their resentment at his trickster ways in their happiness to see another human being, someone who looked as they did and who spoke their language. "You are still alive!"

"Of course I am!" Istavan appeared to have suffered an injury, and his right ear was plastered with an herbal poultice, but clearly it was not enough to dampen his high spirits or curb his ill manners at all. "You didn't really think the Crimson Mercenary would be slain by some common soldier before attaining his destined kingship? My poor young queen, you must have been worried over me."

Istavan bent down to kiss Rinda's upturned face, and was met with a sharp slap of her hand.

"Your queen, indeed!" The girl's face grew red with anger. "I won't tolerate your impudence!"

"Don't be embarrassed. I know you missed me—I saw how happy you were when you spied me coming."

Istavan burst into laughter.

The humans' conversation was largely lost on the Sem gathered around them. The chieftains Ilateli, Loto, Tubai, and Kalto were preoccupied with the arrival of their new allies, the Karoi; they could not hide their relief that the powerful tribe had joined them, but all except Ilateli of the Guro were more than a little anxious as well. The Karoi were famous for their bravery and ferocity, but the ferocity was a double-edged blade; it had brought the Sem a victory but also increased the instability of their tenuous alliance.

"By the way..." Done teasing Rinda, Istavan had grown serious, and now he looked around intently. "Where is he? After all the trouble I went through for his sake, he could at least come and express his appreciation. Does he think he's already been crowned King of the Sem? Kids, what is your leopard-headed boss doing?"

"Guin? He's, um..."

Rinda hesitated, then gave an evasive answer. She didn't

know what Istavan might be hiding or what he had been asked to do, nor did she want to tell him what she knew of Guin's latest plan; she felt unsure enough about it herself. But Istavan, irked by her circumspection, refused to be put off and kept repeating his questions. Rinda looked to her brother for assistance, but Remus wasn't inclined to stand up to the mercenary, and so at last she hesitantly told Istavan that in fact she didn't know where the leopard-man had gone.

"What did you say?"

Istavan's response was much worse than she had expected. He lunged forward as if he meant to grab her by the shoulders and shake her. Rinda quickly stepped back.

"What does he think he's doing, absconding like some court spy and leaving both of you here?"

"Don't say 'absconding'—that was hardly his intention!" Rinda answered angrily. "Guin is risking his life to save us. He went to seek reinforcements because, without them, the Mongauli will drive the Sem into a corner!"

"Reinforcements!" The face of the Crimson Mercenary was a sight to behold. "I swear by the train of the Queen of the Dawn's red dress, I would like to know where he can find reinforcements amid all this bleeding sand! Must be he finally got his memory back and took off for his homeland of leopard-headed freaks!"

"Istavan, you are so heartless!"

The mercenary's lack of manners drove Rinda to distraction, but at the same time, hearing his ranting after they had been separated for a while made her feel a little fondness for him, too. She did not regard Istavan with the same kind of awe that she felt for Guin, but he had nonetheless become a companion—almost a friend.

Abruptly, the princess came to the conclusion that it was best to tell Istavan as much as she knew and not try to conceal anything from him. "Guin took a chance," she said, and explained the leopard warrior's plan to go in search of the giant Lagon. The mercenary listened carefully, and as she went on he made a face as though he had bitten into a mouthful of salt.

"Lagon?" he demanded. "You are saying Guin went looking for the phantom tribe of the savage Lagon? In that case our chances of getting reinforcements are about as good as the chances he'll return with a troop of leopard-headed monsters like himself. By Janos, that is very helpful." The pragmatist's black eyes signaled that he thought the very opposite. "And you say he promised to bring this phantom army here within four days? Doesn't that cat-faced monstrosity realize there are some things he cannot do in this world?"

"You are no different, Istavan of Valachia!" Rinda was furious at the way Istavan had spoken of her protector. "You are always saying that you will do things beyond your ability—it is as if you live in your own dream!"

"She's right," Remus joined in. "You say you're going to find the Shining Lady and become a king."

To the twins' surprise, Istavan didn't respond in anger, but simply winked and smiled. "I may not look it, but I'm a realist," he informed them. "My guardian deity is Ellis, the Goddess of Suspicion, and the blood that runs in my veins is as bitter as the water of Corsea and won't accept the temptation of a dream in broad daylight. The only future I claim is the one I can make possible. I never promise anything I cannot do! And I would never go into the desert to chase a wild idea like... like bleeding *Lagon*."

"I heard you say before that your guardian deity is the Goddess Irana," Rinda replied sarcastically. "It seems like all the gods and goddesses are your guardian deities, Istavan."

"Yes, especially the goddesses. Older women tend to find me irresistible," Istavan answered shamelessly. "But I guess Guin's patron deity must be the blind and stubborn god of hell. And both of you are duck-shaped dulax. I don't understand why you let him go off by himself. If you had just gone with him, you all could have escaped safely, pretending to wander off on some insane hunt for a phantom tribe. It's not like we have some obligation to share the fate of these desert monkeys."

"The Sem saved us!" Rinda drew herself up angrily. "And besides, Ilateli didn't understand that Guin wouldn't desert the Sem—he thought Guin would run away instead of seeking out reinforcements."

"That's why we're here." Quickly Remus explained that the chieftain of the Guro had been unwilling to let the twins depart with the leopard-man.

As soon as Istavan heard the boy's story his eyes narrowed, and his face grew crafty.

"Right." The mercenary licked his lower lip. "I see. Now I understand my hunch that something was wrong." He gnawed at the corner of his mouth, a series of sly expressions shifting across his face. "It was too strange that he left both of you here and just disappeared—after all, you can barely even communicate with the Sem. Now I see why."

"What are you suggesting?" Rinda's voice rose shrilly. Though she found it difficult to get along with Istavan, she realized that he was far more knowledgeable in the ways of the world. His store of experience seemed endless.

"Hey, how many warriors do the Raku have?"

"W-Why?"

As Rinda grappled with the question in confusion, Remus answered for her. "I believe they number between twelve and thirteen hundred."

The princess stared at her brother in amazement, unable to believe that Remus had been able to supply that information. As far as she was concerned, her twin was a blockhead and a sissy.

"About a thousand..." Istavan continued to gnaw at his lip. "How about the Rasa?"

"They have about half that number."

"Ah..."

"What is it? What are you thinking?" Rinda shrieked out, unable to bear the suspense. "Please tell me! Don't tease me at a time like this!"

"All right. Shall I tell you? It seems Her Royal Highness has failed to understand what is happening," Istavan replied sardonically. "Well, your smart brother says that Ilateli wouldn't agree to you and Guin leaving here together. Ilateli is the chief of the Guro—the black-haired monkey-folk you see all around us, looking bigger and nastier than the rest of the wildlings. That means that both of you—and me, too, now, by the looks of it—have been left as hostages. Do you understand what that means?"

Rinda gasped.

"To make it brief, the Sem don't really trust Guin—their precious *Riyaad*. At this point in our little war, our side is pushing forward. But what if the Mongauli army, which has suffered some losses but is nonetheless far better trained than these monkeys, pushes back? At all costs we have to avoid starting to fight amongst ourselves. Even when Guin is here to take command the Sem squabble over whether they will follow him or not. And now, by the pale forehead of the Moon Goddess Aeris, he is long gone!

"He said to wait for four days? Four days? Even one day is doubtful. I imagine the Sem started acting like balto cocks squabbling over territory as soon as he left. But that old monkey Loto wants to protect you. He says that you saved his granddaughter, and he feels he owes you a big obligation." Istavan snorted derisively. "The dull ol' Rasa will be on Loto's side too. The problem is the Guro, those black monkeys—and the Karoi, too, now that they've joined the mix. Hey, those guys are actually respectable soldiers. And right now they're starving for blood. Even I was shocked after I traveled half a day with 'em. Once their blood frenzy gets started, stopping 'em's harder than peeling off sand leeches. I bet the Guro and the Karoi get along very well."

Rinda gasped again.

"I am beginning to think that my return was only part of Jarn's evil plan for me. The Karoi and Guro together are stronger than the Raku and Rasa together—and even if the Tubai came in on our side, the black monkeys are better as soldiers. I don't know what I was thinking, coming here. After I escaped from the valley, why didn't I steal a horse and escape from this forsaken desert? What if the Karoi and Guro decide they can't wait any longer and start to believe more in their own chiefs, who they know can fight for them, than in long lost Riyaad?" Istavan spread his arms wide in a gesture that left the twins to imagine what would happen if that came to pass.

But Rinda wasn't inclined to agree with Istavan's assessment of their wildling allies.

"The Sem have only succeeded in this war because of Guin's help!" she exclaimed. "Without his planning, they would have made a frontal attack straightaway. They wouldn't have lasted for a single day—they would already be exterminated from Nospherus." Rinda gestured dismissively with her hand. "And Loto's not the only one who knows that. Tubai and Ilateli do, too. They're not stupid! And Guin told them to wait for four days..."

Istavan shrugged doubtfully but offered no reply.

Instead, Remus burst out unexpectedly: "Rinda, Guin hasn't exactly gained the Sem's trust by vanishing into the desert!"

Rinda was taken aback by her brother; she had grown accustomed to him following her lead unquestioningly. She stared at him intently, as if she could read in his face what had changed, and he blushed self-consciously. "My, my," she said, "since when have you become so wise?"

"The prince can see what's right in front of him," Istavan cut in brusquely, emerging from a moment of contemplation. "Anyway, if Guin can make it back here a day early—or even half a day—it shouldn't be a problem. But if the time comes and he doesn't show, we will soon be fighting for our lives. And if something else cajols the Sem into fighting amongst themselves before then, it will be a terrific opportunity for the Mongauli...

"And then of course there are the monsters of the desert, which might take things into their own hands—or jaws—at any moment. Sand leeches, yidoh, vampire moss, mouths-of-the-desert... And to think that he's out looking for something that nobody knows how to find! Or maybe Guin does know how. Or maybe not. I wonder..."

"Oh, please stop it! I beg you!" Rinda raised her clenched hands as if to cover her ears. "Please don't talk about the sand leeches and the yidoh. What if something *has* happened to Guin? Then we have no choice but to die here—don't you understand that?"

"Rinda!"

Remus embraced his sister, and the two clung together, comforting each other even as they shared their fears. For a long while Istavan gazed at them in silence. His dark and playful eyes had changed, reflecting some inexplicable mystery; behind them a plan was forming.

"Of course I know that. You don't have to say it," the mercenary whispered at last, his voice taking on a tone the twins had never heard before. Perhaps he was thinking about the two thousand soldiers and one gray-haired old knight that he had betrayed to death, who had died screaming his false name—died in fire and agony, swearing they would never forgive him. He noticed that the twins were looking at him strangely and mumbled something about not feeling like himself before disappearing towards the opposite side of the oasis. Remus and Rinda watched him go without another word.

Despite Istavan's dire predictions, and the twins' ever-growing worries, little more happened that day. Guin did not return, and there were no enemy attacks. In fact the day was unusually calm, and the desert did not seem like the battlefield it had become.

The air grew very hot and still, as if the sandstorm that had passed earlier had taken every breath of movement with it. As the sun rose higher the heat grew steadily worse. There was no sign of a breeze, and the Sem, gathered around the oasis pools, dully soaked their feet and hands. The children and the elders had been sent into shelter to the north, so there were no longer any youngsters running around playing their wildling games. Rinda and Remus kept company with Suni, and together the three rested in the limited shade of the oasis trees, trying to escape from the heat. When the sun finally set and the temperature cooled with characteristic desert swiftness, everyone was relieved. Yet it wasn't long until the pleasant evening coolness had turned to uncomfortable cold—another hallmark of the unique Nospherus climate.

The chieftains of the Sem had all grown quiet and surly, isolating themselves from one another. The hostile mood of the Karoi seemed to have infected them all, and spread in an unfriendly wave among them. Now the wildlings of each tribe avoided associating with members of the other tribes and seemed reluctant even to talk with their own elders and leading warriors. The Karoi themselves—though they had ostensibly come to ally themselves with the rest of the Sem—were the worst of all. They seemed to simmer with ferocity, as if ready to unleash new atrocities at any moment, and even Loto wouldn't get close to them.

This was the state of the Sem army at nightfall. The mixed horde of wildlings, with no overall leader, had lost all semblance of being a unified force. The different tribes had withdrawn into separate parts of the encampment, where they gathered aimlessly, ate simple food, and slept deeply without bothering to post sentries. After a quiet day, and without Guin to lead them, the Sem had quickly grown slack.

So it was that no one noticed when a squad of Mongauli scouts quietly approached the oasis, drawn by the brilliant glimmer of the water reflected in the night sky. The squad stopped cautiously at a distance, and just two or three scouts separated from the main group and crept forward stealthily. They seemed no more than shadows in the darkness, but these were watchful shadows that moved in as close as they dared to the oasis and carefully observed the dispositions of the Sem. Then they slipped back to the squad and were reabsorbed. Tense, whispered voices carried out a quick conversation; the soldiers quietly retraced their footsteps back the way they had come until they had reached a sufficient distance from the sleeping Sem, at which point they galloped headlong all the way back to the Mongauli camp.

The scouts' report was exactly what the Gohran army had been waiting for. The Mongauli ranks parted to make a lane down which the triumphant squad marched to the general's pavilion to make its report. The information they bore had already been sent to Amnelis before the procession arrived, and she was waiting for them just inside the pavilion entrance dressed in full regalia for the coming battle—white gloves, a matching belt, and a long mantle flung back over the shoulders of her gleaming armor. Her lips were taut, and she held her joy in check as she listened to the report.

"This is good news," she said at last. "Feldrik! Carry me a message!"

"Taking the field, I presume," the knight replied and dashed away.

For a moment Amnelis remained gazing at the leader of the scouting squad. She seemed on the verge of making some extended speech, but simply said:

"This is a glorious achievement, Astrias!"

"Yes, my lady."

Astrias's whole body was shaking with emotion. But when he raised his eyes, the general was already striding away.

Moments later Feldrik was addressing the gathered invaders while Amnelis, resplendent, looked on. "Army of Mongaul! Prepare for departure! Our goal is the army of the Sem, encamped in an oasis to the northeast!"

The knight's voice was husky as he continued the general's message.

"We shall launch a surprise attack before sunrise!"

Chapter Three

The Attack

— I —

It was the last hour before sunrise, and a secret tension crept through the darkness of the night. The Sem slept uneasily, struggling with troubled dreams, clutching their stone axes to their chests; often one or another would wake with a low moan, feeling stifled by some unexplained force, and lie fidgeting for a time before nodding off again. The army of seven thousand wildlings was separated into tribal groups gathered irregularly around the oasis like so many fields of dark unquiet fruit, every warrior curled in sleep or crouching drowsily with knees drawn up. Now and then, one of the shapeless black forms turned over suddenly in sleep or stretched its arms and legs, and half-awakened voices scolded it to be quiet. The night air was filled with the distinctive odor of the Sem's small, hairy bodies; an interloper unaccustomed to the smell would have found it difficult to breathe without choking.

Istavan contemplated the wildling army with disgust, feeling depressed that his survival depended on such creatures. They seemed to exist at the boundary between humankind and ape, these Sem; they were a cursed tribe, not human, but not exactly beasts, either—though the time was coming when their animal side would be fully exposed. The sounds of the wildlings' snoring breaths rose up on all sides, mixed with low mutters and whispers, more like the night noises of a band of wandering monkeys than the sounds of a bivouac of soldiers camped on the eve of a decisive battle.

Istavan found that he could not fall asleep, despite his mental fatigue from his tense work among the Mongauli and from the long journey to the oasis in the company of savages whose language he could not speak. His body was exhausted, but his mind would not allow him to rest, and he didn't know why. For a long while he had waited in hope of a brief respite of slumber. Giving up at last, he stood and tiptoed quietly between the sleeping Sem warriors until he reached the edge of the oasis, where he sat down on the root of a desert shrub. Istavan had survived on the strength of his own devices for so long that he never felt lonely or bored when alone, but he had acquired the unwieldy habit of talking to himself, even debating himself and answering his own questions as he brought his private plans to a conclusion. Now he carried on an unconscious conversation as he sat grasping his knees, occasionally toying with his dusty shock of hair, which he had tied up with a copper ring.

"Yeah, that's right—I'm too deep into Nospherus now to strike out into the desert alone, no matter what. My water would soon run out, and whichever way I go I'd be surrounded by nothing but dry sand. I don't know what direction I'd need to take, and even if I did—there are monsters everywhere. No, I wouldn't have a one in ten chance of making it! And what if I tried to go back to the Mongauli? That's not an option either. What if some survivor of that cursed Marus Corps remembered my face? Then I'd have nothing to look forward to but hot iron. Arrgh! This Istavan from Valachia always gets into a scrape! Now I'm left to depend on baseless hopes, like the Sem defeating the Mongauli army. I can't go forward, and I can't go back, by Istar's silver tail! Where is that bastard Guin? Why did he have to go and leave us behind?"

Istavan shivered as if the chill of the night had sunk into his body, which would not have been surprising under the circumstances. Nonetheless he took off his blue knight's gear and tossed it into a campfire that smoldered nearby. Now he was clad only in light boots and a singlet and hose—garb more suitable for the desert day. He hugged his own shoulders like a woman to shield himself from the cold air and gloomily surveyed his surroundings. The endless black undulations of the desert and the brilliant glitter of the stars on the oasis water were all that met his eyes. He shivered again in the coldness of the Nospherus night.

"Arrgh! What kind of evil took my sleep?" He shook his head as he muttered in agitation. "Even when I was imprisoned in Stafolos Keep, I didn't miss my shut-eye, not for a single night—but then maybe there's a reason for it. Hmm. I, the Spellsword, Istavan of Valachia, was given a special extra sense of precognition as a gift for being a dear child of the gods. My neck gets hot and prickly if I'm on a ship that's about to catch fire, and if a patrol's heading my way, I shiver and stop my stealing. I know this to be true. So I had better stay up—there must be some reason why I am so irritated and anxious. Jarn, grandfather of the gods, follows his own reasons. And if that tomboy seer Rinda doesn't feel anything, then it's probably just because she is not much good as a seer.

"Oh, Doal's toes! These Sem stink like monkeys!" he grumbled, and tried to distract himself with his vast treasury of memories. "Ah, how long ago did I drink that whole bottle of fire liquor? How long since I bought that dirty yellow-skinned whore with the great moves in bed? Ha, and how long since I ate that whole rack of boar's ribs with my greasy fingers? Ah..."

Istavan realized abruptly that he was speaking rather loudly, and grew quiet with embarrassment. He threw himself down on the thin grass of the oasis and breathed in the cool green aroma.

"I don't want to think about it, but I have to think about it, and I'm ready to think about it. I'm not a fool. So, what is going to happen to me if Guin doesn't come back? If the Sem lose, and the Mongauli capture me? Ugh!"

He shivered again. No matter how he considered it, the prospects gave him little cause for hope. The mercenary shook his head despondently, then stood and stretched with a rough gesture as if trying to rid himself of negative thoughts. He stopped his movement abruptly, becoming as stiff as a bronze statue before slowly lowering his arms to his sides. For a moment Istavan dropped his gaze, and then he raised his eyes again to make sure that he was certain of what had suddenly seized his attention.

Whatever others might think about Istavan as a man, few could doubt that he had great skills as a mercenary, with more experience than most soldiers twice his age. Those skills served him well now; he did not miss what the darkness would have hidden from a less preternatural observer.

"Well, this is a fine state of affairs!" he whispered with a soft exhalation. His eyes burned with a strange brightness that made them glitter like a jaguar's as he peered at a wall of shifting shadows far out across the sands. "That *is* the Mongauli army, trying to sneak in without lights, muffling their horses' hooves and muzzles with cloth."

Standing poised at the oasis edge, Istavan swiftly considered his options as he studied the black shapes of the Gohran soldiers creeping forward through the night.

"What a fine state of affairs, this! The monkeys don't understand the elements of warfare—not even something as simple as planning night watches. Well, they can't help it; they *are* monkeys. But that leaves me with one big problem to take care of!"

Istavan was well aware that his treachery may have made him as sought after by the Mongauli as Guin and the royal twins. Once again he measured the distance to the approaching soldiers with his eyes; then, he theatrically yawned and stretched before turning and walking with pretended calm back amongst the Sem until he reached the area where the Raku slept.

There he found Rinda and Remus, lost in dreams and hugging one another, lying together with Suni on a spread of furs.

When he drew near to them he said in a low, casual voice, "Hey, wake up. Hey."

He shook the twins gently, but they seemed unwilling to wake.

"Uhh..." Rinda, still half asleep, turned toward him petulantly. "What is it, Boganne? Does my father need me? If it isn't morning yet, please let me sleep. Please..."

"Shit!"

Istavan was getting annoyed, and he shook them again more forcefully.

Finally Remus opened his eyes and complained in a sleepy voice, "What is going on?"

"Hey! I swear, this prince and princess wouldn't wake up if the Mongauli attacked the Crystal Palace at the front gate! Which they did! I beg you, wake up! Please!"

"Okay, okay, I'm awake—what's going on, Istavan? Has Guin come back?" Rinda, who always woke faster than Remus, asked sleepily. Then the meaning of her own words jolted her fully awake, and she jumped quickly to her feet with an exclamation. "Has Guin come back?"

"I beg you, be quiet," Istavan replied sullenly. "The opposite of that. Listen very carefully. The Mongauli are heading this way. If I am not mistaken, they are spreading out to encircle us, and they can probably have this oasis surrounded in no more than a twist. Probably it's their whole army out there—be quiet, I told you to listen to me!"

Istavan grabbed each of the twins by an arm; Rinda and Remus seemed on the verge of screaming. "Probably the Mongauli intend to stage a final battle. Listen, I can't speak

Sem, and I doubt this situation would translate very well anyhow, but Loto can speak a little of our language. Wake him quietly, and tell him what is going on. Tell him very quietly to avoid an uproar among the tribes. If the monkeys get riled up, the Mongauli will realize that we know they're here. Then they'll attack us right away so we have no time to prepare, and that would be just as bad as being caught by a sneak attack. We all know that they're much stronger than us in a direct fight. Surviving this battle is going to depend on how much time we can buy. Make Loto understand this however you can—use sign language if you have to. Make sure he knows that causing a row is the worst thing he can possibly do. Now go and tell him! Oh, and tell him that scouting the Mongauli forces would not be wise either—the most important thing is not to give them any hint that we've noticed their sneak attack. You understand?"

"A-All right, I will try."

Rinda's voice was shaking. In this dark moment the weight of Guin's absence had fallen heavily on the twins. The two gazed fearingly at each other and embraced without words. Roused by the commotion, Suni sat up and looked at the three humans with round, questioning eyes.

"Go, right away!" Istavan hissed at Rinda. "You cannot waste any time!"

"I-I understand."

The princess pushed her brother away, and knelt beside Suni. Hurriedly she began to explain to the wildling girl that she needed to talk to Loto in secret. The twins' ability to converse with the wildings had greatly improved over the past couple of days, since their main diversion while traveling with the diminutive barbarians was studying the Sem language, and they had found plenty of time between the battles in which to practice what they learned. However, their power to convey the relatively complex instructions Istavan had given them was limited by the simple vocabulary of gestures that formed a part of the Sem way of communicating.

The mercenary stood nearby sweating and staring at them with obvious impatience. After a short while he seized the hilt of his sword and turned to walk away. Remus, who had begun gesticulating to Suni alongside Rinda, stopped short and looked at Istavan with round eyes.

"Where are you going, Istavan?"

"I am going scouting," he spoke with uncharacteristic bluntness.

"Oh?" At this, Rinda too paused. Istavan may not have been a warrior of Guin's caliber, but the Crimson Mercenary was now the royal twins' chief defense. "Didn't you say that even scouting would not be good?"

"Sending out scouts would attract attention, yes. So I am

going to do it for you guys," Istavan explained plausibly. "If I get caught, I can make an evasive answer. Tell that to Loto too."

Remus nodded. "That makes sense," he said.

Without waiting for further discussion Istavan hurried away.

Rinda and Remus watched him go, then turned back to Suni. They had finally made the Sem girl understand what was happening, and now they hurried with her to give the news to Loto. None of them stopped to consider why Istavan had volunteered to carry out such a dangerous task. The three did not know of the mercenary's role in the Mongauli disaster at the valley of the Karoi, for Guin had told them nothing of Istavan's secret mission, and for his part the Valachian never said anything that might ever put him at a disadvantage. If the Raku had known of his recent exploits, even innocent folk such as they might have wondered why such a cautious, self-interested man would put himself in the path of a Mongauli army hungry to punish its betrayer. But the twins and their wildling friend never doubted the mercenary's words. Trusting his instructions, they went to Loto as swiftly as they could and did their best to explain to the Raku chief what was going on.

Meanwhile the majority of the Sem remained asleep, oblivious to the stealthy tread of destruction approaching from beyond the oasis. Istavan for his part slipped carefully through the outer circle of the sleeping Raku. He had taken a bearing on the distant crags to the north and was working his way in the direction of Dog's Head Mountain instead of scouting the area where the Mongauli force would soon arrive.

Not even Istavan could sneak away from his companions without a guilty conscience, but he told himself again and again that it was his own life that mattered most. If he needed to fight to defend it, well, his valor could surprise even himself—but there wasn't much point in bravery unless it was strictly necessary. *That's right, Guin's the one who took off and left us behind! Is there any reason why I need to tackle the Mongauli army in his place?* As soon as he was free of the Sem encampment, the mercenary broke into a run, moving quickly up onto rocky high ground. There he found a hiding spot behind a large boulder, and after stabbing his sword into the ground to make sure there were no yidoh, sand leeches, or other creatures concealed there, he hugged his blade to his chest and hunkered down. His intention was to remain there until the battle was over instead of needlessly showing his face to the Mongauli.

Istavan shut his eyes and tried to sleep, but even he could not be so shameless. Behind his eyelids his thoughts seemed to race in every direction, fears and worries mixing with uneasy plans—and always at the back of his mind was the certainty that hiding behind a rock in the Nospherus waste meant the constant risk of encountering the creatures of the desert, a risk almost as great as the battle he was avoiding. It was not long before Istavan found himself shifting around restlessly, anxiously opening and closing his eyes. Finally he decided to remain awake. Absently chewing on a piece of rock moss, he contemplated his circumstances.

"That's right, it's all Guin's fault." He sat up and hugged his knees, trying to justify himself. "If Guin was here, it would be all right, but that leopard decided he'd rather escape by himself and dumped all his duties on me. It makes sense. If I were him, I wouldn't put my life in danger either. *Of course* the reason he took off was that he couldn't carry on his shoulders the heavy load of saving the twins."

Istavan raised his voice argumentatively as he talked. "That's right. It's not my fault! First of all, I am not abandoning the twins. I am merely hiding from the Mongauli for a moment because I would become their most wanted man for the rest of my life if they saw my face now. No matter what I might tell them, if they were to find me, a human soldier, among the Sem who ambushed their blue knights—I hate to think of what they'd do to me! And I didn't even want to betray them.

"Count Marus, if you could hear me! Count Marus, it was Guin who made me carry out the plan! Please, I beg you, if you must hold a grudge against anyone, hold it against Guin, not me. Oh, I didn't hate you! I never wanted your departed spirit following me around! It's not fair...

"Oh!" Abruptly the Valachian interrupted his monologue as a distant sound caught his ear. Freezing where he was, he listened keenly for a moment, then grasped his sword with white-knuckled force as he whispered to himself. "I hear them, I hear them! It's begun! The battle has begun! By the whistling horn of the battle goddess!"

Istavan found that he could not stop shaking. His hiding place became unbearable, and he crept out slowly from behind the boulder until he was crouching in the open. From this new vantage point he could hear the sounds in the distance much more clearly. The clanging of swords, the clack of crossbows, the insect hiss of hundreds of flying blow darts; Mongauli shouts, the neighing of horses, the Sem's characteristic cries—*aieee, aieee, hiaaaa*—like a tide it swept over him, the unmistakable deafening roar of battle, the sounds of the living and the dying. It seemed that the battle had already reached its height, the full Mongauli army throwing its weight against the gathered tribes of the Sem.

Still the night lingered, and Istavan grasped his sword like a cane, leaning on it as he listened intently to the darkness. He wanted desperately to know which side was winning, but his ears alone could not tell him. The screams of the Sem and the Mongauli were intermixed, almost indistinguishable amidst the cries of wounded horses and the crash of metal on stone, until all blended into a murky cacophony of noise. Without thinking the mercenary moved out further into the open, overcome with frustration at not being able to follow the progress of the fighting. Finally he climbed up on top of the boulder that had sheltered him and gazed out towards the battlefield. Yet dawn had not yet broken, and darkness hid the oasis somewhere out in the desert expanse. The first glimmer of sunrise would be sure to show him the rising dust from the fighting and pinpoint where the battle raged, but for now he could see nothing whatsoever, and it was playing havoc with his nerves. Any number of times he jumped down from his rock, on the verge of running off to join the battle, but each time he stopped short in a fluster. His mind was in turmoil, his instincts of cunning, selfishness and self-preservation struggling with a deeply buried streak of kind-heartedness that had unexpectedly emerged.

And so Istavan remained where he was, listening keenly, while his thoughts filled with worry for the fourteen-year-old twins trapped in the middle of the battle. Once again he looked at the sky and realized that at last the night was disappearing. The sky was no longer totally dark—it had changed to an ultramarine color and, little by little, pale light was pushing the darkness away from the east.

Lifting his sword in his sweaty hand he gazed southward towards the battle, as if at last resolved to act—but an instant later he screamed at himself: "Oh, shit! What am I thinking? Istavan of Valachia, you are a fool indeed! Here you are hiding safely. If you sneak back into that battle, how much attention will you get? What has happened to all your ambitions? Your plan to become a king? You shall not die for down-and-out children and monkeys!"

Once the morning came, the situation would be a little clearer—he told himself that. Once the morning came, once the morning came... Surely the light of morn would bring some conclusion to the mortal combat that continued in the darkness. That moment would soon arrive. The dawn would also mark the beginning of the fourth day, the day on which Guin had promised to return by sundown with reinforcements for the Sem.

— 2 —

Hours before the attack on the Sem encampment, the Mongauli army had made its preparations, commands flying swiftly among the ranks as they gathered in the darkness.

"Quiet! Don't make a sound!"

"No talking!"

"Keep the horses silent. Bind their muzzles with cloth so they don't neigh."

"Be careful with those swords. Don't let 'em clang on your armor."

"Soldiers, see that the wheels of those carts are well-oiled!"

Then, even as the orderlies continued to scurry back and forth with last minute directives, the massive force swung solemnly into motion. Astrias rode at the head of the vanguard, with Pollak at his side. Earlier the young captain had volunteered for scouting duty and had had the good fortune to locate the hiding place of the united Sem tribes. For the first time he had won Amnelis's unqualified praise. Now he was as jumpy as a young colt; he knew, as did every member of the grim army around him, that the coming battle would be the final one—or at least it was sure to lead to a grand confrontation.

We won't let them escape again.

We will fight to the finish. This day will be remembered as the day the last Sem fell.

When this battle is over, we will be able to return to dear Mongaul, across the waters of the Kes.

Throughout the army each warrior's thoughts were different, but the mood in the hearts of all was the same. All had heard the orders that outlined the battle plan:

"The entire army will halt before reaching the oasis where the Sem are camped, and separate into two forces. One of the forces will move to the north of the oasis to block the Sem's retreat, while the main force will attack the Sem's encampment from the south side. Captain Irrim will command the blocking force, and he will take care to arrange his soldiers in a wide crescent to prevent any Sem from slipping away to the east or the west as well. In the unexpected event that the Sem become aware of our forces before the deployment is complete, a trumpet will sound. In that case the entire army will attack immediately from the south, but Captain Irrim will drive straight through the Sem's forces, reform his troop, and maneuver to intercept the wildlings' retreat as originally planned.

"It is of the utmost importance that the Sem are given no chance to prepare themselves for the battle. Once the order to charge is given, all soldiers will advance furiously to attack, and destroy the barbarians completely. None are to be left alive, except for the leopard-headed monster, the traitor Eru of Argon, and the twins of Parros—those four shall be taken captive. But all of the Sem must perish. The very shape of the Sem shall be erased forever from Nospherus!"

The wrathful words simmered with the desire for revenge that burned in Amnelis's heart. Yet for all the fury that drove it, the advancing army moved cautiously, its maneuvers coordinated to maintain the advantage of surprise against the Sem. Astrias's red knights rode at the vanguard, followed by the Alvon red who had lost their commander Leegan. Behind them came the subdued black knights of Talos Keep, with the injured Tangard riding in the rear. Vlon and Lindrot led the white knights, Amnelis's direct command, its gleaming ranks still two thousand strong and almost untouched by the fighting. Lady Amnelis rode in their midst with her two runecasters and their portable shrines, with Feldrik's handpicked knights as her personal guard. Next came the badly mauled ranks of the footmen, and then finally Irrim's corps at the rear. These last had to be careful not only to watch out behind them for Sem scouts, but also to be alert for the more monstrous denizens of Nospherus such as the sandworms that were a constant peril.

As the army advanced, the cloth-muffled hooves of the horses raised a dancing haze of dust in the moonless gloom of the desert night. The soldiers marched in silence, afraid lest they make any noise that could draw the attention of wildling sentinels. Like an enormous, mute serpent, the invasion force wended its way through the darkness, trailing a wake of fine sand that hung like a deeper shadow behind them.

Once, the Mongauli troops had formed a mighty army of fifteen thousand, led by eight lord-captains including the renowned Count Marus. But that was before they had left the familiar line of the River Kes and struck deeply into Nospherus, battling strange enemies at every turn. Now Count Marus and Viscount Leegan were dead, and Captain Tangard was wounded, and the army's numbers had fallen to less than ten thousand. Nonetheless they made a proud army as they began their latest journey.

"Did I underestimate Nospherus?"

"Lady?"

Palanquins conveyed the runecasters on either side of the white horse which Amnelis rode; to her left the curtains of one lifted a little to reveal the dull gleam of eyes. A low voice spoke from within.

"Did you say something, my lady?"

"It is nothing, Gajus. I was talking to myself."

Amnelis raised her reins and waved him back. A commander-in-chief should show no doubt or indecisiveness as she rode to a battle, not even to her staff. Such matters could be discussed later, in the privacy of the command pavilion. The lady pulled her visor down and spoke in a bare whisper only she herself could hear.

"This land is as vast as it is barren. Endless sand, and endless stone... It is too vast! If I had more than fifteen thousand—if I had one hundred thousand, or more—it would have been easier. Who could have foreseen such resistance from the Sem? Now little is left of our supplies of food and water. If this desert fighting is prolonged much more by Sem resistance, we will need to fall back to a defensive line. We might even need to consider returning home, but that's the last thing I want, that would make our work here almost pointless. If we retreat, the Sem are bound to regather their forces and escape to the northern mountains. That would destroy our morale. It would be like building a castle in the sand, to see it blown away in the wind."

"Gajus," Amnelis lifted her visor a little bit and pitched her voice softly so it wouldn't carry far.

"Yes?"

"Gajus, what do you think? Do you think it would be wise to send a small troop under Feldrik back to the river to meet the troops waiting there, and return with the reinforcements which should be at Alvon by now?"

"Well..."

"Or should I instruct them instead to establish a supply line? I don't want this difficult campaign to drag on. If we are successful in defeating the Sem this time, we can return to our defense line, and I want to start afresh building a fort. To be honest with you, I'm concerned about Torus. And I am anxious, too, about the crystal city. Count Polan was made proxy commander of the Parros occupation suddenly and without preparation. And right before we left the Crystal Palace, I had begun to see signs that the remnants of Parros's soldiery had established a force of partisans to resist the occupation." Amnelis slipped her hand beneath her helmet and pushed back her blond hair in annoyance. "Yes, all that is making me somewhat anxious."

"Indeed, my lady," Gajus said in a flat contemplative voice. "As to your question... Perhaps the fighting here will all be settled by the time any reinforcements could arrive. And if it is not, then I think that even with reinforcements it would be difficult to exterminate the Sem with their forces scattered across this desert."

"You are saying that it's not necessary to send for reinforcements yet."

Amnelis felt somewhat heartened by his words. He seemed to have drawn conclusions similar to her own.

Gajus continued: "My lady, if you wish at least to send the reinforcements at Alvon a message, you must advise them that the situation is always changing; they would need to be prepared to move at any time. It would be difficult to predict where they should meet us."

"Yes. That's what I was thinking, also. The running battles we are fighting confuse directions rather quickly. Yet it would be wise, at least, to let the backup force know our current location." Amnelis spoke as if in deep thought. "As you know, we have come deep into the interior of this country—we can no longer even see a shadow of the Kes River in the distance. Yet this is only one step into the desert. We still haven't located the valley that Cal Moru speaks of. This wasteland must continue far beyond the stony mountains. Gajus, Nospherus is truly vast."

"Indeed, it is vast."

Amnelis seemed on the verge of saying more, but after a moment she reconsidered, and spurred her horse on ahead. Heavy silence enveloped the command group once again.

The advance continued. The desert spread out before the

army in gentle undulations, like the calm surface of a dark ocean. Even as the Mongauli neared the oasis that was their goal the land did not appear to change, creating a feeling of unreality for the advancing men that was only broken by an occasional shrill shriek or other disconcerting noise. Once, a soldier screamed as he was grasped and pulled under by the long feeler of a mouth-of-the-desert. Another time, a crashing sound broke the quiet as one of the vanguard thrust his spear through a bigeater that had appeared silently from the darkness; the knight pulled his weapon free only to have the bigeater bite it in half with a dry snap and then disappear as noiselessly as it had come.

"Quiet!"

Every time the silence was broken, the offenders were sharply reprimanded, with little sympathy shown even to those who had fallen victim to some monster of the desert. Without realizing it, the Mongauli had slowly grown accustomed to the ways of Nospherus and the strange deformed creatures that prowled its wastes. And so, steadily, the army marched on, jealously guarding its cocoon of quiet. The only sounds tolerated were the low voices of messengers sent by Amnelis to relay orders. Reports of directions and words of encouragement for the soldiers, these murmured messages made no echo in the desert. A strange stillness, like the calm before a storm, had settled over Nospherus. Nights in the wasteland were usually as quiet as death, but on this night in particular the silence was felt keenly by the Mongauli. It carried with it the menace of the madness of battle that was expected before sunrise.

The night march had begun without the moon to light the way, for although the silver orb had risen in the sky, a bank of clouds, unusual in Nospherus, had appeared to hide its cool radiance. For a time the soldiers walked as shadows in the desert. Then at last the changeable Moon Goddess Aeris in her hazy dress peeked from the clouds' darkness to stripe the landscape with bands of pale glitter and wavering gloom. Stars became her little followers, serving also as guides to the watchful knights below. As the Mongauli advanced it seemed to them that the sky drew closer, leaning down as if it meant to fall on them; but despite the strange illusion it never came down to walk among their ranks. Sometimes a wind touched the soldiers' faces, bringing without fail clumps of soft white angel hair to cling to them, but these strange visitations no longer surprised or alarmed the Mongauli troops, who knew the ghostly strands to be harmless, just one more of the bizarre phenomena that constantly reminded any traveler he was journeying in Nospherus. Again and again angel hair landed on men, horses, and their gear, only to melt away noiselessly, leaving no residue behind. The Mongauli paid little heed to these short-lived wind flowers, marching on indifferently as the weird Nospherus night drew down about them.

Astrias rode proudly at the head of the force, knowing that the entire army followed him towards the final battle. Although he had scarcely slept over the past few days, his face was bright and eager, and his eyes peered intently into the darkness; he was determined not to miss anything that might affect the success of the attack, any hint of what was to come—a tiny reflection of water from the oasis, the dim shadow of a sentry ahead. Leading the vanguard was the great chance of which he had always dreamed. Jarn had gifted him with this great opportunity to distinguish himself, and to gain the lady's attention—maybe even her affection. Young officer though he was, Astrias cherished no hope of high promotion, nor did he fully expect to ride at Amnelis's side as consort, although she was two years younger than he—yet not because such ambitions were beyond his means. His father was a count from an old family who in his position as Lord Defender of Torus had gained the trust of Archduke Vlad. Astrias, as the first son, could look forward to succeeding to the peerage, and if he rendered sufficiently distinguished service in the army, he might very well be made General of the Left. His family background, good breeding, and age were all more than satisfactory. Should the archduke decide to solidify his foundation by finding a son-in-law within Mongaul for his daughter, rather than arranging a strategic marriage with some royal family, Astrias would be one of the candidates, along with Maltius, son of Marus—and, had he not fallen, Viscount Leegan.

Astrias tried not to base any hopes on such distant chances, however. It was not that he did not dream about it—he loved Amnelis, his first, unspoiled love, wholeheartedly, with an admiration that was akin to worship. And he recognized his feelings for her. But Astrias was a single-minded, honorable, and earnest youth, and he felt that pining for his lady's love, or imagining a future as her husband, was not only impure, but also blasphemous. Yet no honor that he could receive would mean anything to him if he did not also gain the attention of the beautiful lady. For Astrias, a few words of praise from Amnelis—a smiling "good job" or "great achievement"—far outweighed any compliment or decoration any other could give; even a peerage granted for heroism would have no meaning for him unless it came with the lady's approval. *I want to be a perfect knight for Lady Amnelis. I would die to guard her life. That is the reason I was born, and nothing can turn me from that path.* His young, indomitable passion burned with the purest form of love and drove him on to strive his utmost for the glory of her approval.

It must be through the good offices of Janos that my scouting squad was allowed to find the oasis of the Sem. Fueled by this passionate conviction,

Astrias felt the impatience build within him as the army at his back plodded slowly through the desert on the unsteady, cloth-bound hooves of the horses. His knees clenched tighter against the sides of his charger, and he had to restrain himself from rushing on ahead.

Meanwhile, far behind the young captain of the red, the palanquins that bore Gajus and Cal Moru glided silently on either side of Amnelis, who rode deep in contemplation as if she were alone in the desert. Further back in the rearguard, Captain Irrim thought about his close friend Tangard's pale, bloodied face, scarred by misfortune, and gritted his teeth, his hatred growing. Throughout the ranks warriors of every station found themselves beset by troubling thoughts and secret determinations as the shadows of Nospherus swirled around them.

The Mongauli army halted once during the night march, pausing for a brief break before reforming quickly to press on again.

Onward! Onward!

As they continued their advance, Aeris rode the sky above, slipping in and out of the scattered clouds as if she competed with those on the ground and urged them to keep moving on.

"Time, Gajus."

"'Tis less than two twists of the hourglass until sunrise."

"So soon?" Amnelis bit her lips, and then spoke as though

spitting. "If the sun rises, we lose all that we have gained, and are right back where we started. Is the oasis so far away? Astrias said it was not far from our encampment. Surely we have come far! What..." She looked around as though seeking someone more dependable than Astrias, and then rose up in her stirrups, gazing into the predawn darkness ahead. And there, just at the edge of sight, the faintest of glimmers caught her eye—

"Ahh! Look!" a sudden, quiet hum of voices rippled back from the front ranks as the knights were stirred from their silence by excitement.

"That must be the Sem oasis!" Amnelis announced with satisfaction. "It looks to be a mere gallop ahead. Do you see it? Very well—Feldrik, relay the command! All troops are to cease the advance and prepare for maneuvers! "

"Yes, my lady." Feldrik gestured for an orderly to relay Amnelis's order to his subordinates. A moment later, however, she stopped him short.

"No! Wait for a moment." Suddenly, the lady-general's face betrayed a new tension. She was gazing forward to where two red knights armored in bright crimson were making their way from the vanguard back through the ranks of the main force. They were two of Astrias's aides, and the Lady Amnelis's face hardened.

A little while earlier, at the fore of the vanguard, Viscount

Astrias was nearly dancing for joy as he recognized the familiar features of the terrain.

"Excellent—we are nearly there!"

During his scouting squad's journey back from the Sem oasis, he had overseen the placement of markers to guide the army's return. Pollak had just retrieved the last of these, cheerily jumping down from his horse to seize it.

"This is it without doubt, captain!"

"Good. Gallop back to inform the Lady General. We will prepare our formation to attack immediately." His voice lowered, Astrias leaned forward eagerly and gazed towards the great oasis where he was sure the forces of the Sem still lay in the oblivion of sleep. Yet as his keen eyes swept the scene his body suddenly grew tense.

"Any problem, sir?" his lieutenant Pollak, who had been watching his commander intently, asked in surprise.

"Yes—wait a moment. Something is amiss..." Astrias's voice was heavy with uncertainty. "There is movement among the Sem troops. There is a lot of activity going on! Don't you think so, Pollak?"

"If you say so, I feel—"

"I wonder if they've noticed us."

Astrias and Pollak looked at each other in the darkness. If the Sem had become aware of the approaching army, the

Mongauli surprise attack would be a complete failure.

"Shall we send a scouting party?"

"Yes. But don't use horses. Let them go on foot, and get as close as they can. And hurry!"

"Right away, sir!"

Hustle and bustle quickly spread among the vanguard as the rest of the army began to draw near. Darkness was fading, and the purple hint of sunrise was quickly replacing the black of true night. Swiftly the scouts crept toward their quarry; moments later one of them was already hurrying back to Astrias. With a coughing voice, he reported that there was a great commotion and hurry within the Sem camp.

"Probably they saw us coming, sir. But they seem to have lost their heads. They are running about in all directions within the oasis."

"Hmm..." A look of vexation passed over Astrias's face, but he quickly came to a decision. "They are confused as they prepare for battle. That means they are not ready, yet, and are still vulnerable. Yes! Dispatch the men, Pollak!"

Immediately the lieutenant sent two red knights at a gallop back to the main force to inform the lady-general of the situation. They flew through the white knights like a gale, reined up sharply in front of Amnelis, and leapt from their saddles, barely pausing to bow.

As soon as she had heard their report Amnelis reached her decision.

"The entire army will launch an all-out assault!"

Swiftly the orders spread.

"An all-out assault!"

"Destroy the Sem completely!"

Fiercely a trumpet sounded. Not one among the thousands hesitated an instant as the army sprang into action. No longer were voices lowered or horses held back; the knights rose in their stirrups and lashed their mounts into a charge, spurring them mercilessly. Like a water snake swimming stealthily that suddenly breaks the surface to strike its prey, the army uncoiled in a furious charge, making the desert sands rise up like smoke with the fury of its passage.

"Mongaul! Mongaul!"

Before them, throughout the oasis, terrible confusion spread like a fire in dry grass.

Aieee! Aieee! Alphetto!

Amnelis brought down her baton.

"Kill the enemy to the last soul! Annihilate them!"

Her clear voice pierced the spreading chaos.

3

"It is the enemy!"

"It is *oh-mu*!"

As the exclamations echoed across the camp of the Sem, uncontrollable confusion was spreading as well. It had been already far too late when the twins of Parros carried Istavan's warning to Loto. The Sem, simians that they were, had a far keener sense of smell than any human, and despite the Mongauli efforts to approach in silence, the Karoi, who had been sleeping on the side of the oasis closest to the impending attack, leaped up in violent surprise when the Gohran army approached. At first the warlike Sem had simply gazed about in consternation, sniffing and bristling like brute beasts, and making throaty squeaks of alarm.

Unaware that the camp was waking around them, Rinda and Remus had run to Loto, nearly falling down in their haste, never guessing that Istavan had heartlessly left them to their fate while he sought safety for himself. When they reached the Raku leader they had launched into a painstaking effort to communicate the situation to him as clearly as possible, but they had barely begun their explanation when the encampment broke into chaos around them. Gripped with fear, they turned to stare mutely into the darkness to the west. Something was happening at the outer edge of the oasis. Suddenly, piercing screams and shrill voices filled the air, mixed with the noise of hundreds of feet running. Loto's wise old face quickly took on a grim expression.

"Siba! Siba!"

In answer to Loto's yells, a young Raku soldier ran up, flushed with desperate excitement. The young Sem did not even seem to be aware of Rinda and Remus standing nearby, nervously holding hands. He pointed into the darkness behind him and began jabbering in a piercing voice, but the twins could understand nothing that he said. Loto screamed something back at the young warrior.

"Alphetto!" Loto screamed again, naming his god, his voice changing as if he had abruptly become enraged; then he rose to his feet. Although he stood no taller than Rinda's chest, he carried himself with the dignity of a chieftain and his presence projected authority. Quickly Loto issued a series of commands, and by the time the disturbance the Karoi started had spread through the rest of the camp the Raku were rushing into action.

The Sem were desert savages, unfamiliar with even the most rudimentary practices of strategic warfare. So it was that they had failed to post sentries around the oasis during the night; nor had they made provisions for a skirmishing force to protect the encampment in the event of a sudden attack. Now, although they possessed better night vision than the Mongauli and they had quickly located their human foes, they lost their heads at the first sign of the unexpected onslaught. Many found that they had lost their weapons as well. Like frightened rodents in a box they rushed about, shrieking abuse and trying to snatch armaments from each other as they tripped over those who had managed to sleep through the racket. The Sem leaders shouted out a constant stream of commands in an attempt to restore order, but their efforts were in vain. Istavan's advice, that the wildlings should betray no knowledge of the sneak attack and pretend to remain asleep in order to gain time to prepare for battle, had been given to no purpose. Had Guin been present he might have calmed the Sem and put their troops in order by the shear force of his leadership, but Loto didn't have the same kind of influence over the other chiefs. The Karoi in particular were independent and high-spirited and didn't cooperate well with the other Sem; the black-furred wildlings were quick to action, however, and now, just as they had been the first to grasp the situation, they overcame their confusion faster than the others. In a matter of moments their pride at being recognized as the great warriors among the Sem spurred them into readiness. While Loto was still listening to the news, the Karoi were already gathering up their axes and poisoned darts.

"Ayeeya!"

At the command of their chief Gaulo, without pausing to form any sort of battle formation, the Karoi streamed forth from the oasis.

"Follow the Karoi! Attack the enemy!" Ilateli screamed, and the Guro rushed to battle as well, with no thought of tactics or organizing their forces.

Realizing that they had lost the element of surprise, the Mongauli wasted no time in beginning their assault.

"Charge!"

"An all-out assault!"

Amnelis's commands kept flying. Astrias Corps was at the apex of the triangle formed by the advancing army, and the red knights urged their horses to a wild gallop, swiftly covering the remaining distance to the oasis. The opposing forces were now so close to each other that attempting to set traps or study each other's maneuvers—even firing a volley of crossbow bolts—had become meaningless. The Sem and Mongauli simply crashed together and fought face to face, the two forces intermingling like contending waves. Horses' hooves kicked sand into the air and drawn swords clanged against armor and saddles. In a matter of moments the main body of the Gohran army had reached the outer edge of the Sem encampment.

"Captain! The Sem are heading straight for us!" Pollak hollered.

"Impudent monkeys!" Astrias's voice was feverish as he shouted his reply. "We will crush them! Hold nothing back!"

The hairy mob of Sem rushed forward, brandishing their axes. With a chorus of frenzied squeals they launched themselves against the Mongauli.

"Aiiieee! Ayeeya!"

"Hiaaa! Hiaaa!"

The peculiar, brutish screams that the Mongauli had heard so many times before once again filled the air.

Astrias unsheathed his sword. "Attack! Attack! Attack! Destroy and conquer!"

The Sem enveloped the front ranks of the Mongauli like a swarm of insects and hurled themselves upon their foes. Some of the wildlings leaped high in the air, pouncing onto the knights' war horses, dodging the Mongauli blades and smashing down their stone axes upon their foes' heavy helms. Others attacked from below, hewing at the horses' legs with their axe blades or blowing poisoned darts up into their enemies' eyes. It now appeared that the Sem's counterattack had been prepared much more quickly than the Mongauli expected. Instead of the expected rout, a sea of violent confusion, surging in every direction, had developed in front of the oasis. Now the warriors of the Raku, Rasa, and Tubai had joined the battle as well.

"Aiiieeeya! Ayeeya!"

"Mongaul! Mongaul!"

"Hieee!"

The Sem may have looked like tiny black ants attacking massive, armored locusts, but as they rushed into the fray they showed no sign they had been badly surprised. They fought as a single, wild horde; there had been no time for them to paint their faces before the battle began, so their tribal allegiances were nearly indistinguishable in the darkness. Like countless waves they hurtled from the oasis to meet the longswords of the advancing knights, screaming out madly whether they sank their weapons home or tumbled down, stricken, upon the sand.

"Irrim Corps—forward! Irrim Corps—forward!"

"Cut off the Sem's retreat!"

"The enemy force is unexpectedly small!"

One after another the orders flew, and the main body of the Mongauli force took the shape of a wedge and began to drive deeper into the oasis while Irrim's corps moved out from its position as rear guard. Irrim formed his troops into a broad crescent-shaped line and began to circle around the wildling camp to intercept any retreating Sem. The Mongauli knew they no longer had the strength to pursue their enemy further into the desert interior of Nospherus, so an escape now by the Sem would cost the invaders dearly. Irrim understood the importance of his mission and he urged his men to hurry past the battle that had sprung up before them.

"Cut through the oasis! Form up in the passes beyond!" the captain of the black bellowed. "Crossbowmen, forward—footmen, deploy! Close off every pathway through those rocks!" Irrim pointed out a stony crag for his men to use as a landmark—the very crag where, unbeknownst to them, Istavan was hiding.

Meanwhile Astrias, at the forefront of the fighting, was frowning in puzzlement even as he swung his sword to right and left.

"Pollak!"

"Hiaaa!"

A Karoi warrior appeared suddenly through the predawn gloom, leaping onto the head of the young captain's horse. Astrias pulled back sharply on the reins and cleaved the wildling with his sword, then spurred his mount into a jump to avoid the flailing stone axe of the dying Sem. Without losing his composure, the captain of the red called again for his faithful lieutenant. Pollak had kept his horse close beside Astrias's as the two cut their way through the attacking mob.

"What is it, captain?" Pollak was using his sword like a spear, skewering one Sem after another as they hurled themselves against him. Sticky blood gushed from his foes as he impaled them, and his face had turned red under his helmet from a sudden splash of gore. He spat out some curses and sat back on his horse as he wiped his face clean with the edge of his mantle.

"Don't you think it's strange the *monstrosity* isn't here?"

"Do you mean the leopard-headed man?" Pollak had shared his young captain's dislike for Guin from the beginning. The thought brought something else to his attention, and he looked right and left before speaking. "Yes, and have you noticed, sir? I think the Sem's main force is still in the oasis. Probably he is with them there."

"And he's not the only one—I don't see Count Marus's betrayer or the twins of Parros either. They must be keeping back among the inner ranks of the barbarians. If they were out here they'd certainly stand out."

"They must be in the oasis." Pollak noticed with a surge of worry that Astrias had focused singlemindedly on finding these particular foes and had left himself vulnerable to the fighting close at hand. He spurred his horse closer to call out a warning. "Captain, your back!"

"Oh!" Astrias spun in his saddle and furiously cut down a Sem who had snuck up from behind to target him with a poisoned dart. Yet even as blood spouted around his blade his attention drifted once more. "The oasis..."

The night was giving way to dawn. The sky had gone from purple to indigo, and now a lightening blue, with a line of pale brightness at the horizon. Now the Sem were clearly visible, with their bared yellow teeth and bristling black and brown hair splashed with blood. Astrias gazed out at the maelstrom of battle. The scene was truly chaotic—like a swarm of locusts struggling with a nest of ants—human soldiers mobbed by Sem warriors, Mongauli knights riding their horses over the savages as they cut them down. The Sem fought incoherently, without leadership or tactics, and the result was confusion for both sides.

"Pollak!"

"Yes, sir!"

"Let's head for the center of the oasis."

"Yes, sir!" Pollak raised his head and whipped his horse forward, signaling the advance.

Quickly the red knights showed the skills developed by their hard daily training, overcoming the nearby Sem and gathering their horses around their captain.

"We will charge the oasis! Our targets are the leopard-man and Eru of Argon!" Even as he spoke Astrias saw Irrim's troops beginning to move past, through the outskirts of the battle, and let out a triumphant yell. Then he turned to look behind him and saw white mantles among the helms of the red knights and the dark hair and sun-tanned skin of the leaping Sem; it had to be Vlon and Lindrot, at the fore of Amnelis's command, come up to support his own corps and the remnant of Leegan's. *Victory is inevitable. Our Mongauli army cannot fail to defeat these poorly equipped savages. Unless there is some unforeseen counterattack, or they have made some cunning plan, we are going to carry the day with a simple frontal assault.* Astrias grinned with satisfaction under his visor.

"Hear me, knights of Mongaul! Let us make this day the last day of the Sem!"

"Aye!"

Astrias heard his men cheer with approval and dug in his spurs.

"To the oasis!"

With their captain in the lead, the corps of red knights galloped through the chaos at the forefront of the battle and pressed on into the oasis. Sem warriors rushed at them from right and left in an attempt to halt their advance.

"Ayeeya!"

"Aiieee!"

Masses of the simian wildlings gathered on the approaches to the encampment, waving their stone axes threateningly. The red knights urged their horses to still greater speed and whirled their longswords overhead.

"Yaaaa—!"

A band of Karoi fell with heartrending cries as they were caught and ridden down by the sturdy hooves of the horses.

"Get out of my way!"

Astrias spurred on his horse with ferocious vigor, taking the first path he found into the oasis. A body of knights followed close behind him. Soon they were galloping past an irregularly shaped shallow pond filled with brownish water and surrounded by trees and a dense tangle of underbrush. As they neared the thickest part of the brush they found that the Sem had awaited their arrival and laid an ambush there; the wildlings opened fire with their blow guns, unleashing a fatal hail of poison darts at the red knights at the head of the column. The darts hissed through the air like the breath of a snake; Astrias pulled down his visor and lay his head alongside the neck of his horse to protect his face, but did not slow his pace.

"Kyaaa—!"

A Sem's fanatical scream ended abruptly as Astrias's sword struck home. The wildling fell back into the water at the edge of the pond, a fountain of blood spraying from his split skull to dye the stagnant water. Other red knights fanned out on either side of the path, some riding their mounts noisily right into the pond, wasting the water that was so precious here in the barren desert. The horses' hooves pulled up mud and sand from the pond bottom and churned the waters into murky, roiling waves that soon turned crimson from the bright blood of the dying Sem.

"Hiyaaa!"

"Aiieee!"

The Raku threw aside their blowguns and leaped to attack with stone axes. Astrias gazed about wildly while trying to keep his attention on the Sem. Guin remained uppermost in his mind—he could not forget the insult the towering warrior had dealt him—but he did not spy the striking leopard-headed figure anywhere. Neither could he find the double-crossing false blue knight. The only figures in sight were the small hairy things running through the grass of the oasis, screaming in their strange voices as they attacked. Something suspicious was going on, and the shadow of doubt settled uneasily on the young captain. *They're not here? It cannot be—that would mean this is not the Sem's main force. But there are some thousands here! Surely there can't be too many more of them...*

"Watch out!"

Astrias heard Pollak's cry of warning and his well-trained body reacted instantly, ducking to avoid a stone axe by a finger's breadth. Then as the primitive weapon whistled past he adeptly changed the direction of his horse even as he split another little skull with his sword. *Is he plotting something? Is he directing these monkey-folk from some secret hideout while he plans some sinister counter-stroke an ordinary human couldn't even imagine?* He could not get the anxious thought out of his head.

"Guin!" Astrias roared. "Guin, where are you?" He galloped across the narrow end of the pond and up the far bank, streaming with water. "Are you hiding, you coward? Come out and fight with me! Astrias is here! Astrias from Alvon is here to challenge you! Guin! Where are you?"

The captain of the red gazed about almost desperately, looking like a man searching for a lost lover who has vanished inexplicably. Behind him, the battle had spread across the oasis, red-armored knights and brown-haired Raku splashing through pools of water or crashing through the undergrowth as the dead and dying colored the leaves with their blood. Suddenly Astrias's eyes were drawn by a group of Sem gathered in a cohesive group around a tall tree near the edge of the oasis. Some of the wildlings' most skillful warriors appeared to be protecting this band, for they had slain several knights who rode against them. The group seemed to be trying to make its way towards some safe haven off the field of battle. As he watched, Astrias saw a sudden gleam of white hair amidst the dark-furred bodies. *That is the Sem's leader!* The knight settled his grip on his longsword.

"Mongaul!"

I won't let them escape! Astrias flicked his horse with his whip and sped toward the Sem band. Hurriedly Pollak gathered some of the finest knights of the corps to follow him.

"Follow the captain! Don't let him ride alone!"

With a loud cheer the knights galloped after Astrias, but he paid them no heed. The only thing that filled his mind was the burning desire to perform some heroic act. If Guin and the traitor were not present, he wanted at least to have the chief of the Sem for himself. He also wanted to be there if Guin should appear suddenly out of hiding, leading a band of elite Sem warriors in a surprise attack. With sword held high he galloped forward as though he could outrun his churning thoughts. In a moment, consternation spread through the group of Sem as they noticed his approach.

"Kyaaa!"

"Aiieee!"

"Alphetto! Alphetto!"

Astrias, clad head-to-toe in red, crashed into the band of Sem with the terrible energy of a demon. Back and forth he rode, gouts of blood, shrieks of pain, and the agonies of death following behind him. The diminutive warriors who tried to stop his charge were knocked down and trampled under his horse's hooves or kicked screaming into the air.

There were signs of turmoil around the base of the coconut palm where the core of the Sem group had gathered. Astrias saw some of the warriors there spread out to form a protective circle, while others closed ranks about an ancient Sem with grayish-white hair, urgently trying to lead him away.

"You will not escape!" Astrias screamed as he turned his horse and headed straight towards them. Then he noticed two more figures moving under the protection of fleeing Sem. *Those are humans!* In the new light of the morning sun, his keen eyes fixed on platinum blond hair and a pair of slender, smooth-skinned bodies among the hairy shapes of the wildlings. He felt a sudden surge of elation lift his heart. *I've got them! Those are the Pearls of Parros!* He had seen the twins once before, when they had been captured by Amnelis by the River Kes and brought into the lady's pavilion to face her. That single, brief encounter had left a vivid impression. *If Guin and Eru of Argon aren't to be found...* To recapture the twins would be a worthy and honorable exploit. Astrias turned from the leader of the Sem and raced after the fleeing children.

"There they are! The twins of Parros!"

Astrias heard Pollak's shout behind him and gritted his teeth with annoyance. He wanted to catch the twins with his own hands and bring them back to Amnelis.

"They are my quarry!"

Even as he shouted the words Astrias began to bear down on the twins, spurring his horse on mercilessly and scattering Sem on all sides. Any wildling who tried to oppose him he swatted aside with the haft of his spear.

"Out of my way!"

The Sem, though quick on their feet, could not compete with the speed of a horse on a flat straightaway, and Astrias and his men quickly caught up with them. In a thunderous rush the knights overran the wildling band and wheeled around to attack again. When the twins saw their foes begin to turn they tried to change course as well, and head back towards the oasis; but by now both troops were intermingled. Many Mongauli had been unhorsed in the first clash. In a moment a swirling melee developed as the two forces fought hand-to-hand at close quarters.

"Rinda!"

"Remus!"

The twins called out desperately to each other. A great

warhorse had come up between them and was keeping pace with them as they ran—Astrias's charger.

"You shall not escape!"

Astrias was half crazed with his desire to carry out some famous exploit, and in his fervor he had totally forgotten about the order not to kill the prince and princess. He raised his longsword to slash down on the boy running beside him. Remus saw the blow coming and dodged to avoid it, feeling the wind of the blade pass over his head; he darted to one side and ducked around a trio of Gohran knights in the twinkling of an eye. But in the speed of his sudden maneuver he lost his balance, and slipped and fell headlong on the grass.

"I've got you now!"

Astrias drew a rope from his saddlebag to bind the young prince, but his horse, overwrought and frothing at the mouth with the madness of battle, reared up suddenly and raised its hooves to trample on the boy. Unable to get away, Remus cowered in fear as his doom descended.

"Remus!"

With a scream Rinda sprang past the rearing charger and rolled toward her brother, her long platinum blond hair flying as she sheltered the boy from the horse's milling hooves with her own slender body. With voiceless rage she twisted to glare up at their attacker.

"Ah!"

Astrias exclaimed sharply and lost his hold on the reins. His horse rose up still further, until it stood straight on its hind legs, and with an inarticulate yell Astrias tumbled ungracefully from his saddle. He fell hard, and his horse veered away and left him there. But in a moment the young captain was moving again, oblivious to the pain of the fall and the embarrassment of losing his mount in the presence of his best men. He pushed himself up from the ground and rose halfway to his feet, then choked and grew still, staring raptly at the girl who had just brought about his fall.

And what a girl she was! Her gleaming hair was mussed up and falling about her dirty face, which was pale with exertion and the gripping tension of battle. Despite the chaos around her she remained poised and defiant, sheltering the fallen Remus, seeming to will that no enemy hand would touch her brother even if she must die to stop it. She stared unflinchingly at Astrias as if her gaze could become a flaring blast furnace, ready to burn to cinders any who dared the blasphemy of touching the royal twins of Parros. Astrias flinched in the face of her passionate dignity, overwhelmed by the majestic presence of this fourteen-year-old queen. For a moment that seemed an eternity, they remained frozen, their gazes locked.

Then Astrias rose, ignoring his fleeing horse, and reached

toward the prince and princess. The twins moved more quickly, however, and before the young knight could grasp them they jumped up, took each other's hands, and took off running faster than desert rabbits, dodging the many outstretched arms that tried to seize them. They were cornered no more.

"Catch them! Don't kill them! Those are the twins of Parros!" Astrias bellowed, and behind him he heard Pollak's shouts echo his orders.

The captain of the red felt breathless and stupefied. He stood holding his sword but seemed to have forgotten about chasing after the twins himself. Somehow, to his great surprise, his heart had been shaken by something he could call admiration. One after another, red-armored horses streamed past him. Gradually he came to his senses and stirred himself to locate his steed. Spotting it, he hurried to its flank and climbed back into the saddle. But still he felt as if his eyes were pierced by Rinda's burning gaze, a fire he could not resist, flaring to burn him down.

—— 4 ——

"Rinda!"

Remus was screaming breathlessly as he ran, his feet tangling in the hunched roots of the desert grass. Again and again he nearly fell headlong.

"Rinda—Rinda! Ah!"

"Remus!"

Rinda's cheeks had grown red and her chest was heaving; she clutched at her side, which was cramped with a painful stitch. But there was no way they could stop. Everywhere they turned, reaching hands extended to grab them, and the air was filled with rough shouts, cries of "seize them, catch them!" and the frightening echo of horses' pounding hooves. The twins were powerless, fleeing like rabbits before a ravening pack of red wolves. Rinda's proud heart was burning; as a legitimate royal successor to Parros's throne, running away filled her with shame. Pride, however, would not be enough to bring about a miracle and call down the wrath of the heavens upon her coarse pursuers.

"Ohh... Rinda, I can't run anymore!"

"No, Remus! Run!"

"It's hopeless! We'll never get away!"

"Remus! What are you saying? You are to be king of Parros! We cannot give up now!"

The two screamed at each other at breathless intervals. As they ran, traumatic scenes replayed from the tragedy of the Crystal Palace: their parents and chief vassals slain by the same nemesis that hunted them now, the king and queen's blood shed in the royal hall that had so long known peace and nobility. *I won't die. I won't die. I won't be killed by Mongaul. I will restore Parros—Parros!*

At some point the twins had lost hold of each other's hands. Remus had hurt his ankle in a fall, and little by little he was dropping behind his sister, his voice calling out to Rinda with increasing difficulty. But Rinda did not dare to turn and look behind her as she raced madly onward. She had passed through the grassy ground surrounding the oasis, and now was in soft sand where it was difficult to maintain her pace.

"Ahh, Guin! Guin, help me! Guin!"

Without realizing it, Rinda was calling out the leopard-man's name as she ran. She had begun to stagger.

"Come to us! Help me, Guin! Oh, Guin..." She had placed her last hope on the leopard-headed warrior—if help were to come, surely it would be from Guin, and no other.

Suddenly the girl heard her younger brother cry out sharply behind her. A moment later Remus shouted at the top of his voice. "Run, Rinda! Get away!" The young prince, who had been steadily losing ground, had finally lost his footing and been captured by the Mongauli.

"Remus!" Rinda screamed frantically, but still she couldn't bring herself to turn around, and she kept staggering onward. Somewhere deep in her mind she knew that her best chance was to keep on running, that perhaps somehow she could still escape and come back later to rescue her brother with the aid of Guin. *Guin.* She focused on the image of the leopard-man. Guin would be able to help her. Under his aegis, she could expect any miracle to happen. Hadn't he saved them from the burning ruin of Stafolos Keep? She had not realized just how much she needed that strangely shaped, mysterious figure. If Guin were here, he would swing his big sword with his big strong arm and lead a unified Sem army to shield her and her brother.

If only...

Rinda's eyes grew hot with tears. But this was no time to succumb to emotion. If she could make it into the stony hills she felt she might escape. She must not think of the Sem or contemplate her younger brother's fate—not now, when sorrow could destroy her. A rabbit pursued by the hounds of the god of death, she must flee at any cost. The voice of doubt that told her, *You cannot run anymore*, was suppressed now by the memory of the devastation behind her and her own burning will to live. But her body's strength was failing; she tottered pitifully as she kept on, moving ever more slowly.

And then suddenly she realized that she could barely hear the shouts of pursuit behind her anymore. The smoke and flying sand of the battle, the screams and spraying blood of the Sem no longer surrounded her. It seemed that the red knights of Mongaul were no longer chasing after her. Strangely, the change didn't ease her fears—to the contrary, it gave her a numbing sense of terror and confusion.

Then her feet slowed, and she staggered and finally stopped. Unconsciously she slowly lifted both hands and covered her mouth—and screamed. Or rather, she thought she did, but no sound came. Her sight grew dark with a vision of fear, and her last strength left her. She could only gaze with a hollow expression at the forbidding knights, clad in black, that appeared to rise up from the desert to block her way. Her knees bent slowly, and she toppled over on the sandy ground, both hands still covering her mouth.

Irrim's contingent of black knights didn't approach to pick up the exhausted girl who had collapsed before them. They held their positions, waiting unharmed in a great crescent for the main force of the Sem to arrive. Rinda felt as though a giant black wall blocked her way with ruthless intent. Then as she lay she glanced behind her and saw a single horseman approaching quietly, his charger's hooves raising no dust from the sand. He was a red knight who had removed his helm to reveal his intent young face. For a moment she felt an insane hope grow in her heart.

"Istavan!" Rinda exclaimed without thinking—but even as she found her voice she realized that she was mistaken.

With his black hair, black eyes, long face, and dark complexion, it was easy to imagine that this man was the resourceful mercenary from Valachia and that he had slipped past the Mongauli pickets to come rescue her. There was a difference about this knight, however, and it was a difference that appealed to her: both dignity and youthful innocence showed on his elegant face. Especially in contrast with the wall of black knights in their shadowy armor, the lone red knight shone with a brightness that was almost magnificent.

"Of course..." Rinda muttered absently, her voice trailing away to nothing as her mind reeled on. *Of course he would not come. Istavan could never save us now.* She had worried about Istavan after the battle started, wondering whether he had joined in the fight or if he might have been captured while scouting. When she had realized that he would not return to rescue her and her brother, she had grown desperate; as the Gohrans closed in she had clutched at the hope that Guin would reappear. That hope too had apparently failed her.

The red knight slowly drew closer, riding his horse carefully through the soft sand, and halted in front of the princess. He reached his hand down to her. Rinda flinched away reflexively and gave him a glare full of withering animosity.

Astrias was perplexed. "You know that you cannot evade us any longer," he said hesitantly, unsure of how to treat one who had both the dazzling dignity of a queen and the pitiful vulnerability of an unprotected orphan. "Come over here."

"Do not touch me, Mongauli!" Rinda exploded. "I would rather bite off my tongue and die choking on my own blood than be taken by my foe!"

Astrias shook his head in puzzlement. His mind was working quickly, trying to decide what to do if she continued to defy him.

"Your brother was caught, and taken," he told her, almost apologetically, and reached out again to take the girl by the arm.

Rinda shook off his hand.

"I will walk by myself."

"That is better."

Astrias felt a touch of relief as he watched Rinda stand up and brush the sand from her clothes and hands, but a moment later his unease returned.

"Ouch!"

Rinda winced as she took a step. In the frantic effort of her flight, she hadn't noticed that she had sprained her ankle slightly with a misstep in the soft sand. Now she found that it was uncomfortable to put weight on it.

When Astrias realized her injury, he reached out timidly, as if to coax a stray mountain cat. "Come, ride on my horse," he said.

"No. I have no wish to throw myself on my enemy's mercy."

"It is not mercy. The battle continues, and I must return to the battlefield. This is an order."

After a moment's hesitation Rinda submitted resentfully to the knight's request, and Astrias put his prisoner, still bristling with hostility, in front of him on his horse and headed back toward the oasis. Rinda clenched her teeth, not wishing for her enemy to hear her softly crying, and held tightly to the horse's mane. Astrias fought to maintain his composure; any who saw his face would have guessed he had taken on more than he could handle. He did not venture to speak again. Carefully the red knight made a wide detour around the Sem encampment, where the battle was still raging, and headed for Amnelis's guard.

Suddenly a tiny figure sped toward them from the outskirts of the oasis.

"Rinda!"

With a shrill, eager shout the furry shape leaped up towards the horse. Astrias's sword whipped out reflexively, but it was Rinda, not the tumbling Sem, who shrieked out in agony.

"Suni!"

Rinda tried desperately to jump from the horse, but Astrias's iron grip held her tight. Still she struggled wildly for several moments; then, when she realized she could not get loose, her horror subsided into a chill stillness. Slowly Rinda turned her head and stared very intently at Astrias's face, as though committing his features to memory.

"You killed Suni." Tears were running freely from her eyes, but the princess spoke with perfect calm. "Mongauli are murderers. Mongauli killed my father and mother, and now Suni, my friend. And Mongauli will kill me and Remus. I wonder how long you can hide your crimes from Janos?

"I will never forget your face."

Astrias met her stare sullenly, offering no reply. There was nothing he could do now even if he did give her an answer.

Instead he maintained his silence, and with no more resistance from Rinda he rode on with her until they reached the white knights.

Astrias had hoped to receive some word of praise from Amnelis when he returned with his prize, but the headquarters was still busy issuing orders and nursing the wounded, and the lady-general had no time for him. With a bleak disappointment welling up inside him the captain of the red turned his horse quickly to gallop back to the field of battle.

Rinda was taken by a group of guards and brought to where her brother was being held; there her ankles were tied together like his. The twins called out each other's names as they were reunited, and then simply hugged each other close without speaking. Remus was sobbing, but Rinda steeled herself against her sorrow. Her tears for Suni's passing had already dried, and now, as she held tight to her brother, the slender, high-spirited girl kept her lips pressed shut, swallowing the lump that kept rising in her throat, forcing herself not to yield to emotion.

Rinda could not remember how many times she had been captured lately. Until now, she had always trusted in Guin's ability to rescue her. But this time, the towering, indomitable leopard-man had not arrived to save the day. Even wily Istavan was gone. This time, the twins were all alone. Out on the desert the Mongauli were shouting heartlessly and running down the little Sem with their horses as if they were enjoying some cruel game. Rinda bit her lip until it almost bled. *Guin, where are you? The Sem are lost. Guin... You are the only one. Guin.*

The pitched battle around the oasis was drawing to a close. From the beginning of the war for Nospherus it had been clear which side would have the advantage if the two armies ever clashed directly in an all-out fight. Although the Sem had great quickness and agility and knew every acre of the desert terrain, there was a big disadvantage to fighting with stone axes and poisoned darts against the steel longswords and heavy armor of trained human knights. Moreover, the Mongauli soldiers had begun to grow familiar with the simians' style of combat and had learned to counter their tricks. They had discovered that wearing their helmets with the correct tilt would deflect most poison darts, and that if they parried the stone axes with their swords they could reduce the force of their blows in half. In this battle they had a further advantage, for the fight around the oasis took place largely on ground that was grassy and relatively hard, much better terrain for cavalry than the loose sand of the open desert where the horses' hooves often trod false. As the morning wore on, the elite Mongauli warriors were cutting down the brave Sem one after another. The wildlings fought with tremendous gusto, and the Karoi and Guro in particular had inflicted many casualties on their foes, but it was not enough to outweigh the Mongauli's inherent advantages and the momentum of their surprise attack.

"Fall back! Fall back!"

Finally the chieftains of the Sem shrieked out the order to retreat, and their drums sounded out the message to withdraw. The chieftains gathered their warriors about them and began to slip back into the embattled encampment. But by now it was too late to make a stand inside the oasis.

"They're going to surround us!" Illateli screamed in his high-pitched voice. "They want us to gather into one group! Scatter and run in different directions—deceive them and hide yourselves!"

"Aiieee!" the Sem answered him with a wild cry, and scattered to escape, scurrying like the progeny of a spider caught in a storm wind.

"Don't let them get away! We must not make that mistake again. Exterminate the monkeys without mercy!"

The message was spread through the Mongauli ranks, and the troops spread out to surround the oasis, trapping the Sem within. Irrim's footmen were waiting for the few wildlings who managed to evade the main army and flee towards the stony hills, and they descended upon them in the passes.

Meanwhile, old Loto was hemmed in at the oasis with the surviving members of his bodyguard. His trusted protector, the brave young warrior Siba, was searching for a means of escape.

"Loto, I have an idea."

Siba's eyes were bloodshot as he hurriedly went through his possessions. In a moment he found what he was searching for.

"I was thinking about what Riyaad would do if he were here."

Loto kept his silence and gazed at Siba as the younger Sem took a fruit of smoke plant out of a bag and handed it to his Raku subordinates. He kept a bottle of vasya oil for himself.

"Let's go!"

"Ayeeya!"

The group of Sem let out a wild scream and charged towards the edge of the oasis where the Mongauli soldiers seemed fewest. As they neared the enemy lines Siba's warriors hurled a smoke plant fruit ahead of them, and the desiccated fruit burst open with a loud noise and released a cloud of dense, black smoke. The Mongauli drew back as the inky cloud roiled toward them. Swiftly Siba turned the oil bottle upside down and sprinkled its contents all round, then drew out a flint and struck a spark to the scattered drops. As soon as the oil caught fire, he poured more oil onto the blaze and screamed, "Quickly—this way!"

He urged the old chief onward as the oil-fed fire rapidly

spread. Soon the members of the small band were slithering forward on their bellies like snakes, with Siba out in front throwing smoke plant fruits one after another to create a screen.

"Don't let them go!" Mongauli knights shouted as they rushed into the noxious cloud, coughing and stabbing blindly with their swords.

"Be careful! Don't let them escape!"

Using the rolling smoke as a precarious shield, Siba and about ten other Raku warriors were escorting Loto through the Gohran lines.

"Gather at Devil Rock!"

"Karoi, Guro, Rasa! If you escape, gather at Devil Rock!" the Sem screamed to each other in a language unintelligible to the Mongauli. Indistinct answers came back from here and there amidst the chaos, but no wilding dared pause to form further plans. They ran in different directions to escape from this oasis of death.

Irrim's blocking force, bearing down from the north, and Vlon's troop of white knights, hurrying in from the west, were drawing closer to each other like two heavy doors swinging shut. When they met, the circle of the besieging forces would be complete, and the Sem's retreat would be cut off. But if the Sem could manage to escape once more into the desert, they might yet evade their adversaries' heavy mounted troops and regain the initiative.

"Run, run, run!"

Siba screamed until his voice became hoarse as he sped through the underbrush at the outer edge of the oasis.

"Run, Sem, run! Run, Raku, Tubai, Rasa! Run in zigzags until you reach Devil Rock! Throw them off the trail!"

Suddenly Loto, following close on the young warrior's heels, screamed and halted abruptly.

"Suni! Dear little one!"

In an instant Siba turned and scooped up Suni's body without waiting to determine if she was wounded or dead, or had simply fainted; without missing a step he kept on running. Now the wildlings faced their ultimate race for survival, a final, furious effort to escape from the red iron god of the underworld to the goal of living free and preserving the Sem race. Siba was not the only one who led a desperate band trying to avoid the Mongauli encirclement and pursuit. Running battles had flared up all over the oasis; brave warriors had rallied to aid the leaders of each tribe, gathering in close-knit groups to protect their chieftains—or in the case of Ilateli, following their chief as he led the way, driving a fierce skirmishing wedge into the midst of the Gohran cavalry. The sun had passed its zenith and begun its slow descent, and still the battle commenced before sunrise had not reached its conclusion. As swiftly as the flowing blood dried under the intense rays of the sky's golden orb, it was replenished by fresh gouts pouring onto the hot sands of the oasis.

And then, finally, the encirclement was complete; the Mongauli had the Sem completely at their mercy.

"Finish them!"

The relentless supreme commander waved her hand as if it were a blade.

"Don't let a single barbarian escape alive!"

All at once the conflict ceased to be a battle and became a massacre, a heartless one-sided slaughter. The Sem who had not managed to slip through the Mongauli lines, and the brave ones who had foregone any chance of escape to remain alongside their chiefs, now felt the full might of the Mongauli army. Fierce-faced men with flashing swords rode down the wildlings one after another. The wounded were trampled by the horses' hooves. Those who resisted were cut down piecemeal, and their blood seeped into the waters of the oasis.

Soon the pool had turned a sickening red, and the plants that grew around them were stained with dripping crimson. The groans, screams, and cries of anguish seemed endless.

Chapter Four

THE MARCHES KING

— I —

"Ohh-yee..."

"Aiieee!"

"Yeee-aaa..."

Voices calling out to each other echoed faintly around Devil Rock, which cast a long shadow in the fading light of sunset.

"Are you all right?"

"Did you get hurt?"

The Devil Rock was a large, strangely-shaped upthrust of stone that rose from the rocky lands near Dog's Head Mountain, well to the east of the oasis where the battle had taken place. The Rock was not the only unusual crag in the area; other great formations crowded the desert there, rising in every sort of weird and fantastic shape, and now as the light of the sunset dyed them red they looked like a gathering of deformed giants. In the stillness they shadowed a more diminutive gathering that was assembling at their feet: limping, wounded, grief-stricken little ape-men, the survivors of the Sem, who were now utterly defeated.

"Where is Kalto? Was he killed?"

Under Loto's orders, Siba of the Raku was trying to organize the defeated wildlings; they were walking among the remnants of each tribe to look for the chieftains.

"Tubai? Tubai of the Tubai?"

"Tubai was killed," a young warrior from the tribe answered heavily. Tubai, the yidoh keepers, were decimated. They had been few in number even before the battle, and had suffered heavily in it.

"Kalto is here."

"Oh, Kalto—you are all right!"

Among the Sem tribes, the Raku and the Rasa had always been closest. Loto heaved a sigh of relief and reached out to embrace his old friend.

"Kalto is safe. But many of the young of Rasa were killed," Kalto said with his dirty, bloody head hanging.

"It is the same among the Raku."

"The Raku have the fewest injured," Kalto answered sulkily, unwilling to receive that sort of consolation. "The Rasa are totally destroyed."

"That is not true! Some day, you can have more children and raise them up strong."

Kalto would not listen. "Many of the Rasa's women died." The chief sat down behind a stone and began to grieve with loud, sad cries. "Everybody died!"

Siba shrugged and, leaving Kalto to abandon himself to his grief, went back to work.

"Guro? Guro?"

"Is Ilateli safe?"

"No," a young, heavily-built warrior of the Guro tribe, with wounds on his hands and legs, spoke up as his fellows were wrapping his injuries with herbs. "Ilateli died. *Oh-mu*'s red devils and white devils split Ilateli's head in half. Ilateli fell down, and a horse stepped on him. The white matter was running out of his head."

"Ilateli has died..." Siba hung his head. The powerful, courageous leader of the Guro had been a source of inspiration to the rest of the Sem. "Tubai and Ilateli have both died."

"For the Guro, Ilateli's son will act as chief until we can choose a new chief at our next gathering."

A very black Guro stood up beside the big wounded warrior. "I am he," he told Siba. "I am Utari."

"Utari. How many Guro were killed?"

"Many." Utari spat out the word.

"I am still alive," someone declared in a rough, commanding voice, and it made Siba lift up his head.

"Oh, Gaulo!"

It was the chief of the Karoi. He had been wounded in the shoulder, but otherwise he appeared to be in good health and high spirits, and his ferocity was in full flood. Siba was impressed.

"You made it through the army of *oh-mu*!" Siba didn't like Gaulo, but he could not help expressing his admiration at the feat.

"We, the Karoi, have already destroyed one of the *oh-mu*'s castles. We didn't consider this much of a predicament," Gaulo replied with exaggerated self-assurance.

Siba counted the number of Karoi around Gaulo with his eyes and then returned to Loto.

"Ilateli and Tubai were both killed. Gaulo and Kalto are safe. Not even half of the Guro have survived. The Tubai are almost destroyed. The Rasa are down to the number of a single clan. The Karoi made it through quite well—and the Raku, too. Many have died, but many have survived."

The Sem had only a vague conception of numbers, so Siba's report was imprecise, but he had described the essential truth of the situation. Before the battle, the united tribes of the Sem had numbered roughly seven thousand. In the space of a day's bitter fighting that number had been reduced to two or three thousand.

Loto nodded, and stared around Devil Rock in silence. They had made it past the stubborn pursuit of the Mongauli and escaped to this hidden meeting place; they were unlikely to be threatened again by the invaders' army for a while.

"I wonder how many of the *oh-mu* have died," Loto said in a low voice.

"Not even half of them. Only one *oh-mu* was killed for every three or four Sem."

"Hmnn..." Loto sank into a grim contemplation of the situation. It seemed hopeless, and it was still getting worse.

The Sem had fallen into a state of abject misery. Two of the five tribal chiefs were now gone, and the losses among the warriors had been tremendous. Among the survivors almost all were wounded. They were disorganized and scattered now, resting here and there among the rocks. Even most of those who were moving around the gathering treating the injured warriors bore injuries of their own. The badly wounded were crying and screaming constantly, and when their cries grew too loud the healers stuffed their mouths with herbal medicine to quiet them, fearing that the noise would draw the enemy's attention. There wasn't enough water in the makeshift camp, for most of the wildlings' water bags had been dropped or broken during the escape. There was no food. The Sem knew the desert as only lifelong desert-dwellers could, and some of the more vigorous among them had been given orders to go out and forage for things to eat, but there was little hope that they would find what was needed; worn out as they were, they could not travel far.

"Loto."

"What is it, Siba?"

"Are the *oh-mu* looking for us?"

"Hmnn..." The aged, white-haired face of Loto held an expression of bitterness as he considered this worrisome prospect. With so few warriors left, it would be hard to form even a small skirmishing force to face the several thousand troops that remained to the Mongauli army.

"We must flee farther away!" another voice put in suddenly. Siba gave a start. Kalto, leading some of his best warriors, had appeared suddenly on Loto's other side. He stared intently at the old chief. "We must split apart into five tribes again, and join up with the females and children who have been hiding in the mountains. Then we must find a way farther east, or north into the high mountains, and conceal ourselves somehow until the *oh-mu* have gone. There is no other way for the Sem to survive."

"No! That is no good!" In spite of his low rank, Siba could not help blurting out a response. "The *oh-mu* have no intention of leaving any of us alive. They made sure to finish off everyone who had fallen. The *oh-mu* intend to eliminate all of the Sem and wipe us from Nospherus. If we divide ourselves, they will slay us one tribe at a time no matter where we hide."

"Is this young one the successor of Loto?" Kalto asked with a grimace.

Loto nodded vaguely, and spoke with reluctance.

"Perhaps they do not seek to kill us all. I do not think they would kill those who surrendered, if it came to that. And Nospherus is huge. Once we are in hiding they will not be able to find us so easily."

"Nospherus is vast. But even we Sem do not know every part; there are places where we, too, are strangers," Siba pointed out. "The areas we know—they will be able to find us there eventually. The areas we don't know are very dangerous. We don't know every secret the land holds. Once we leave our territory, we won't know where the colonies of sand leeches or the valleys of the yidoh are. Who can say how many Sem would be lost if we try to make a new part of Nospherus our home?"

"We can think about that later," Kalto said dismissively. His foul mood was clear in his scowl. "Battle is sure to bring death, and the Rasa don't want to add any more to the numbers of our dead. Rasa is a small tribe. If any more of us die, Rasa will be extinct. Loto, if you do not wish to hide or escape, what are the Raku going to do? You do not hope to fight with the *oh-mu* anymore—or do you? The Sem cannot fight any longer. The Sem don't have the strength to fight even sand leeches, now."

"I—" Loto had just begun to speak when he was interrupted by a sudden exclamation.

"We must fight!"

The voice was high, young, and female.

"Suni, dear one..."

Siba rushed to her side. The little Sem girl had accosted them unobserved, her head and shoulders painfully wrapped with herbal poultices. She had listened to the conversation in silence, leaning weakly against a boulder.

"This is Suni, my granddaughter," Loto explained to Kalto's subordinates. "She was stabbed by a red devil. We found her fallen, left for dead."

"Grandfather, Rinda and Remus were taken by the *oh-mu*!" Suni's high-pitched, birdlike voice was shrill with emotion. "Please save them. Before the morning comes, please go back to the *oh-mu* camp and save them!"

Siba caught the frail body of the Sem girl as she began to topple over, and helped her to sit.

"Little Suni... You are weak. You must be careful."

"They saved Suni—this time, Suni must save them!"

"Suni..." Loto lifted his hand, discomfited.

"That's right! Riyaad said the Sem must fight to survive. He said that we had to continue until the sunset of the fourth day, and we would survive. If we did that, he would bring reinforcements. And Riyaad doesn't break his promises! He will come back by tonight. We need to fight a while longer and lead the *oh-mu* astray, to keep them confused until the day is over, until Riyaad is back. Riyaad will be back to save us!"

"Oh Riyaad..." Loto whispered, remembering.

Kalto was furious.

"You want the Sem to hold out even now, when the *oh-mu* hunt us? When the day has ended, the Sem will be gone from the face of the world!"

"Grandfather, please save Rinda! Siba, please save Rinda! I beg you!"

"Both of them are *oh-mu*—the sister and the brother," Kalto objected. "*Oh-mu* don't kill *oh-mu*. But *oh-mu* kill Sem. To save two *oh-mu*, is it right to kill many Sem?" He turned to the wildlings who stood behind him. "Tell me, is it right?"

Angry cries of "Yaaa!" and "Yeeyaa!" answered him from many mouths.

By now most of the remaining Sem warriors had gathered around Loto's rock to listen to the debate.

"*Oh-mu* kill *oh-mu*!" Suni screamed indignantly. "Suni was locked in the *oh-mu* castle. Many *oh-mu* were killed by other *oh-mu* and beaten by them with sticks."

"Because *oh-mu* are evil," Kalto stated simply. "We should not sacrifice Sem to save evil *oh-mu*."

"If we don't fight, all the Sem will be wiped out!" Siba interjected. "Those who die fighting sacrifice themselves to save the rest of us!"

Loto remained silent, still sunk deep in thought.

"Fight!"

"Save Rinda!"

"Hide, as quickly as possible!"

Siba, Suni, and Kalto screamed as if they were trying to drown out each other's voices.

"Don't shout so loud," Loto told them gravely. "If the *oh-mu* are near enough to hear, the Sem will be exterminated before they have a chance to hide or fight."

The arguing wildlings lowered their voices, but it was clear that none of them had changed their opinion.

"Fine. If the Raku want to fight, go ahead and fight," Kalto spat. "The Rasa will take the Rasa's path."

"Just like that!" Siba clenched his fist. "We have too few warriors as it is, and without the Rasa..."

"Rasa cannot afford to lose more."

"We need to fight to survive!"

"Rinda saved Suni!" the wounded girl put in.

"Then the Raku are the ones who need to repay the debt.

The Rasa don't have anything to do with it."

"Kalto," Loto said with calm solemnity. "Your mother's mother is my sister."

Kalto fell silent. Loto turned and slowly surveyed the crowd. With the weight of uncertainty upon him, he looked like an aged, white monkey with doubt and wisdom mingled in its eyes.

"Sem of the Guro. Who succeeds Ilateli now that he has passed?"

"I, Utari, son of Ilateli," the powerfully-built young Guro answered immediately, and stepped forward from among the gathered wildlings.

"What is the will of the Guro?" Loto asked.

Utari hesitated; bold as he was, it seemed that he was not yet used to the authority of his new position. He turned and looked at his fellows. Whispers were coming from the crowd of Guro.

"The Guro are...ah..." Utari mumbled uncertainly, shuffling his feet. It appeared that he didn't know how to answer in a way that would inspire the hearts of the Guro as their leader should.

"Ilateli said we had done enough," an older Guro spoke up from behind Utari. Murmurs of agreement rippled quietly among the Guro.

"No! Ilateli was the bravest of the brave. If Ilateli was still here with us, I have no doubt that he would tell us to defeat the *oh-mu*," Siba countered passionately, not caring how his remarks would be received. "He was no frightened weakling to show the enemy his back during a battle!"

The Guro appeared to be unsettled by Siba's words. Utari shifted his gaze between Kalto, Loto, and Siba, but said nothing more. It seemed that a turning point had been reached.

"Loto! I have something to say," a deep, rough voice broke in suddenly, so harsh that everyone was startled.

Loto stepped forward a little. "Gaulo," he answered simply. He had not anticipated the Karoi chief's intervention.

"The Karoi know nothing about the promises made by the *oh-mu* named Riyaad. We joined the Raku and Guro in this fight because we received messages from Loto and Ilateli, and also because the *oh-mu* came to destroy our village. But the Karoi don't remember any promise to save unknown *oh-mu* children or to become the lackeys of Loto and Riyaad."

"Gaulo, listen to me..." Loto tried to interrupt, but the fierce-faced Karoi leader ignored the dignified old chief.

"The Karoi want to hear Loto's explanation. Loto's messenger said that fighting alongside the Raku would drive away the *oh-mu*—that this was the only way for the Sem to survive. That is the reason the Karoi joined the battle. But now we are still arguing about whether to fight or run away. Did you trick the Karoi, Loto?"

"This is no time to demand explanations!" Siba shouted angrily. "Loto is not the one who is wrong. This war would have gone differently if the Karoi had joined us earlier. Last night, if the Karoi had detected the *oh-mu*'s sneak attack, many more could have escaped. But an ally does not ask an ally for explanations after losing a battle."

"No one is talking to you, young one," Gaulo answered insultingly. "I am asking Loto."

"The promise made by Riyaad," Kalto began to speak with renewed vigor. "What has happened to Riyaad anyway? Where is the *oh-mu* who was with Riyaad? They didn't leave to bring back reinforcements. They left us fighting with the *oh-mu* so they could escape and survive. Those two children plotted together with them! We cannot trust *oh-mu*—not any of them. Riyaad said to wait for four days. Those four days have already passed. There is no sign of Riyaad coming back. There is the proof."

"Wait," Gaulo snorted derisively, "what of his promise to return in four days? The Karoi were not told about that."

"Listen, and you will hear what happened." Reluctantly, Siba explained Guin's promise to the Karoi chieftain.

Gaulo's ugly face grew distorted with a sneer as he listened.

"Wait for four days? The Lagon will come to save us? Hah!" he yelled, his fury growing with every word. "What kind of child's tale—leaving hostages! Hah! Gaulo of the Karoi should have been there. Not even a fool would dare to make Gaulo such a stupid offer!"

Utari stirred uncomfortably.

Siba could not hold his tongue. "The Karoi don't know Riyaad! Riyaad has helped the Sem. Riyaad is no coward and would never run away by himself and leave the other *oh-mu* behind. If Riyaad said he will bring reinforcements, he will bring them. With Riyaad on our side, even if the *oh-mu* had ten times our numbers, we would win in the end."

"Loto," Gaulo snarled through clenched teeth. "This inexperienced one makes so much noise we cannot have a conversation. Anyway, the Karoi cannot put their faith in stupid tales of reinforcements, brought by some child of Alphetto born in answer to our prayers. Such tales do not answer the question of why we Sem have to risk ourselves to save two *oh-mu* children. If they are *oh-mu*, let *oh-mu* save them. If not, leave them. The Karoi have finished what the Karoi came to do. The Karoi will follow the path of the Karoi."

"The Guro, too—the Guro are going with the Karoi," announced Utari, urged by those who stood behind him. He seemed flustered as he spoke.

Kalto stepped forward into the momentary silence that followed. "Let's hide in the mountains."

Loto met Gaulo's stare calmly and spoke with an air of self-possession before Siba could pitch in. "I see. The Karoi wish to run away without losing their heads. The Karoi don't have the energy to fight against the *oh-mu* anymore."

"What are you saying?" Gaulo's voice began to rise, but in the next moment he broke into a smile. "I won't be fooled by your trick. The Karoi don't know the one called Riyaad. If he has made promises, let him keep them; it is no matter to us. We will do as we will. If you try to stop the Karoi, they will make their way by sheer strength."

"Gaulo!"

Loto stepped forward, and Siba's body grew tense. The young warrior and several devoted followers crowded close behind the Raku chief, gripping their stone axes. Immediately the Karoi who stood with Gaulo poised themselves for violence, holding their darts at the ready.

Threatening sounds like the growling and snorting of beasts filled the air; all at once the Sem were reduced to bristling animals facing off with all the ferocity of their wild nature. Their upper lips curled up and they bared their teeth. Siba edged closer to Loto, wanting to protect his chief. If the Rasa joined with the Karoi, the Raku would be left to fight alone against four tribes—the Karoi, Guro, Rasa, and Tubai. Even though these others were all at least as badly depleted as the Raku, together they formed an overwhelmingly superior force. Siba was undeterred, however; he still believed fervently in Riyaad and was determined to hold out for him no matter what. To Siba, it was not possible that Riyaad would abandon his friends to save himself. A low growl leaked from the young warrior's mouth. Very slowly, Loto lifted up his hand in a calming gesture, as though he meant to speak again.

Just then a Raku warrior ran up, staggering from exhaustion.

"Loto! Danger comes! *Oh-mu* are coming here, bearing fire! They are searching for the Sem."

Loto had learned his lesson after the attack the night before, and this warrior was one of the perimeter sentinels that he had placed around the new camp at Devil Rock. Now the Raku chief wasted no time getting to the point.

"Where are they now?"

"There are many torches moving in the desert. They are probably less than half a day away by foot."

"Gaulo, Kalto, Utari," Loto commanded briskly, "let this arguing cease! Gather all your warriors immediately, and let us go to Dog's Head Mountain."

"Dog's Head Mountain? But there's a pack of terrible

wolves that lives there," Kalto started to disagree, but shut his mouth abruptly when he realized that this was no time to argue.

"This does not mean the Raku are giving up on fighting the *oh-mu*," Loto added calmly. "Anyway, I will still need some time to devise plans."

"Do you mean to do that on your own? Or have you put all your trust in the one called Riyaad? Are you still waiting for the *oh-mu* who abandoned us so he could escape?" Clearly, Gaulo had made up his mind about the leopard-man.

"We will see," Loto replied, unruffled, and turned to give an order to one of his messengers.

As he did, a second watchman came running from the edge of the camp.

"*Oh-mu* are coming this way! There are many!"

Tumult gripped the Sem as the news spread among them. Worn out as they were, it seemed they would not be permitted a single night of rest.

2

The Sem lost no time in gathering what little they had and leaving Devil Rock. By now night had fallen completely. The eerie, heart-freezing howls of wolves sounded in the distance, borne on the winds that came down from the mountains. Even for the Sem with their excellent night vision the stony terrain made for difficult walking; still, the wildlings dared not use any lights to guide their way. If the Mongauli were to catch them here and now, there was no doubt that the tribes of the Sem would be destroyed to the last warrior.

The wildlings called out to each other as they moved, and those who marched at the outer edges of the group probed the ground ahead with long sticks—a technique, learned during their long years in the desert, that helped to frighten away many creatures of Nospherus before they could draw too near. Angel hair was blowing on the wind, coiling and twining around them, but the eerie floating substance was becoming less plentiful as the wildlings drew nearer to the higher crags. When they looked behind them the Sem could see many flaming torches spread out across the desert, like the lights of a fleet of fishing boats out to sea. It seemed that the Mongauli were arrogant after their victory at the oasis; they were no longer concerned about concealing themselves but wanted instead to push forward at top speed to find any Sem warriors who had survived the battle. Clearly they believed that their opponents no longer had the energy to fight back. The progress of the torches, like stars drifting across the desert, might have appeared dreamy and beautiful to a casual observer, but for the Sem the restless flames looked more like the fires of hell, flickering with the menace of impending death.

"If Riyaad were here..." Siba mumbled. "If Riyaad were here, without doubt he would order us to slip back close to the torches, and make a sneak attack to forestall their advance."

"And if we did that, we would all be destroyed." Gaulo had overheard Siba, and sneered in his powerful voice. "Evidently the creature called Riyaad desires us to be wiped out completely. But the Karoi don't want to get mixed up in Raku business. We would not obey a fool's orders."

"Then why do you still follow us, and not take a different path?" Siba snapped back at him.

Gaulo shrugged his shoulders.

"That is funny. The Karoi thought the Raku were helpless and wanted to be with the Karoi. The Karoi are not afraid of *oh-mu* at all."

"Are you saying the Raku are afraid of *oh-mu*?" Siba's voice rose, and he was bristling. But he regained his self-control when Loto chided him.

"Don't open your mouth. Focus your mind. We will soon arrive at Dog's Head Mountain. If the *oh-mu* realize that, it will be the end of us."

Suni was walking by Loto's side. She was clearly suffering from her wounds, but she bore up bravely through the pain and offered no complaint. Siba glanced at her little figure and felt a sharp pang of pity. Then he looked ahead again, and saw Dog's Head Mountain looming before them. He knew that many fearsome creatures would be lurking there—creatures worse than wolves, some worse even than the monsters of the desert. The Sem had already entered the foothills of the mountain, and the land was rising in uneven ridges, but the mountain itself was still a little distance away, so they could see its strange dog-shaped silhouette clearly. Siba, who was anxiously contemplating the various hazards that would await them once they approached the towering peak, suddenly came to a realization.

"This is the Dog's Head Mountain, where Riyaad was heading," he whispered excitedly in spite of himself. "If Riyaad came here, we are getting close to Riyaad."

Meanwhile the Mongauli were drawing nearer. It was unclear whether or not they had noticed the Sem, but it was obvious that they had come eastward to hunt for them.

The Sem talked amongst themselves as they marched, discussing whether they should change direction to try to shake the Mongauli off their trail. The lights of the pursuers were still fairly distant, and it was impossible to determine if they had realized the Sem's location, or if it was just a simple coincidence that they had sent their scouts in the Sem's direction to search. Yet even bull-headed Gaulo didn't suggest changing direction. If the Sem turned aside now, they would be heading away from the mountains into barren regions where the terrain offered no cover of any kind in which they might hope to hide. After their defeat it seemed natural to all the Sem to seek for a place of concealment.

"Suni, dear one," a worried Siba called out to the girl as she staggered along. Wounded as she was, Suni was also showing signs of exhaustion and was increasingly lagging behind. "Suni, are you in pain?"

"I am all right. It is nothing!" the granddaughter of the chief asserted bravely. Siba knew that it was only her courage talking, but he felt a little relieved nonetheless. If Suni were to fall too far behind, Gaulo would insist that she had become an encumbrance and probably suggest that they abandon her or even kill her out of mercy. Siba kept an eye on the girl, wondering how long she would be able to keep going. It was not long before he noticed held-back tears shining in her eyes.

"Little Suni. Truly, how are you feeling?"

Suni shook her bandaged head eloquently and gave Siba a pleading look as if she wished to cling to him. After a moment she said in a low voice, "Siba, I want to help Rinda. Please help Rinda."

"Suni, dear one..."

Siba was at a loss. He was a loyal Raku warrior, but he also admired Riyaad deeply. He had no objections to helping the twins whom Riyaad held in such high regard. Loto was his chief, however, and Loto had no intention of going back—not now, at any rate. It was clear that the tribes would need to settle down for a while before any daring action could be undertaken; Loto needed to talk to Gaulo, to calm him down and win him over, and then perhaps they could think about what could be done for the twins. Right now Gaulo's faction didn't care about two *oh-mu* prisoners. Siba shook his head powerlessly, and Suni pressed her hand to her mouth to keep herself from crying.

Once again the howling of desert wolves drifted down from

the mountain crags. It was a sad and terrifying sound, a chilling music that made the hair on the Sem's backs stand on end.

"...I report that our losses amount to three hundred and sixty-two dead, one thousand five hundred injured, and a few dozen horses killed," the messenger's toneless voice sounded in the desert night. "The deaths were almost all among the footmen, and the majority of injuries were caused by stone axe blows to the head or poison darts to the eyes."

"The number of casualties is higher than I expected." Amnelis was sitting on an ornate camp stool in front of her pavilion. She wore a satisfied look as she toyed with a whip that lay across her lap. "Still, the losses they suffered were far greater than ours—beyond comparison."

The oasis had become a scene of gore in which every breath brought in the overwhelming reek of blood. A gruesome pyramid had been built with the severed heads of the Sem; their headless corpses littered the ground. The groans of their wounded had been replaced by a grim and final silence.

The Mongauli army had separated into two forces; one had left to pursue the fleeing Sem warriors, while the other went through the oasis to finish off the survivors. When it had been determined that no more Sem remained alive, this second group quickly reformed its ranks, sent messengers on ahead, and prepared to join the pursuit.

The advance force tracking the remaining Sem kept their comrades at the oasis updated with a constant stream of messages regarding the ape-men's whereabouts.

"Sightings of Sem in the direction of the mountains."

"The remaining barbarians have escaped into the hilly terrain to the east; it appears they have established an encampment there."

"It is believed that the Sem are now heading into the rocky area at the foot of Mount Pherus."

Amnelis listened attentively to each message as it arrived and responded with rapid-fire orders. "Don't let them think we are pursuing them too closely. If we let them separate and scatter into the desert it will be difficult to round them up. Slow the pace of the pursuit—let them think that they've escaped, then give them a while to gather and regroup. Once they have assembled we will strike them again. Don't let any of them, not even one, escape alive. Am I right, Gajus?"

"Yes, my lady," the runecaster answered in a dull voice, gazing out at the lady from under his hood. His grim solemnity contrasted sharply with the keen air of the lady-general whose high spirits had returned.

"General, it will be trouble if they get up into the rocks on the mountainside," Vlon worried.

Still enjoying the taste of the Mongauli victory and the capture of the twins, Amnelis let his objection pass without becoming angry.

"Of course, I have thought about that. I won't let them climb the crags. Scout out the approaches—find their paths up onto the mountain—but remain out of sight. Let them think that they have a safe escape route there, but see to it there is a force waiting in ambush at the mountain's foot. It will serve our purposes perfectly: a one-way path, with no way out. It will be their undoing. Am I right, Gajus?"

"Certainly..."

"But don't let them suspect what we are doing. To ensure that they're taken by surprise, let our main force ride with flaming torches, moving slowly to corner them. Meanwhile the holding unit will go on ahead. The main force's action will be primarily a diversion; it's the ambush that will do the job. The leader of the holding unit will be...Astrias. He performed well when he captured the twins of Parros. Irrim let too many of the Sem leaders escape." Amnelis, feeling unusually garrulous, favored her subordinates with a pointed comment. "I didn't expect that from you, Irrim. I told you to be sure those escape routes were closed off, but you let the wildlings slip through like water leaking from cupped hands. It's a good thing you have a beard—your face must be red with embarrassment."

Captain Feldrik of the white knights flinched uneasily at the general's words.

"Very well," she went on, her humorous mood passing. "We will set the trap during the night. Until then, we will merely follow the barbarians—not too close and not too far. We must not lose sight of the Sem, or make any obvious move that will reveal our plans. If anyone compromises this surprise attack, I will have him beheaded! See that Astrias is informed of his new command."

"Yes, my lady!" Feldrik hurried to deliver the orders.

"This operation took much longer than I expected," Amnelis turned and spoke more quietly to Gajus. "Now finally it will be ended. And after that, before searching with Cal Moru for the lost valley, we will establish a forward camp with a garrison of troops, and the rest of us will return to the River Kes to rest and re-supply. Gajus, divine a propitious day for our return home."

Softly, Amnelis laughed.

The lady's high spirits had affected her aides, and Vlon and Lindrot joined in her merriment. If Count Marus had still been alive, he might have spoken up and checked the young general's indiscretion. *Amnelis—it is not yet the time to relax. I am proud of you for your success, but what is this about runecasting a date for our return? Thinking ahead is the job of a leader, fine. But it is too optimistic to believe that*

everything will go as planned: no plan is certain until it has been made real. It is too early to relax your hand from your sword. Please, don't grow incautious. Do not forget that teaching of Alzandross's Book of Tactics*: "A war is not ended until the last soldier falls."*

Count Marus was not there, however. Beginning with Feldrik, the white knights who served as the general's aides did not dare correct her moods; instead they spent every moment catering to them.

Amnelis spent a moment lost in thought, gazing around absently as she twisted a strand of her long, shiny blond hair around one finger. The sun was setting across the desert, and darkness was gently laying its shroud upon the scene of blood and death around the oasis.

"Prepare to move immediately after sundown. Upon my signal, all soldiers will light flaming torches and begin to advance eastward along the path the Sem have taken. We must give the wildlings no hint that part of our force is elsewhere. Instruct the captains to spread the marching columns into broader formations, to cover more ground and make our numbers appear greater than they are. Astrias's unit will maneuver separately, and I trust that, this time, none of the Sem leaders will escape." Amnelis paused, and then with a faint smile she added, "Consider this an order for the Sem's execution."

"Certainly, my lady!"

The Sem following Loto had no way of guessing the fate Amnelis had prepared for them. The path to Dog's Head Mountain was long, and their progress was slow in the darkness. If they had dared to light their way they would have been able to advance through the rugged terrain more easily, and torches would also have helped to protect them from dangerous creatures such as stone-mimics. But in their fear of pursuit they did not dare call attention to themselves. Meanwhile, the flickering torches that followed behind them only heightened their anxiety; it was as if the Mongauli were mocking them, and the flames urged them forward. The fear of the desert wolves and the pain of wounding their feet on jagged rocks in the dark were as nothing compared to the terror of the Mongauli pursuit. Dog's Head Mountain was tantalizingly close, but their journey seemed to be prolonged endlessly by the rocky ridges and defiles that crossed their path.

Kalto asked once to pause for a rest, but Gaulo told him coldly, "If you want to take a break, only the Rasa will take a break."

After that, even Suni did her best to give no hint of fatigue.

The incessant howling of the wolves also caused the Sem great distress. The desert packs seemed to be waiting eagerly for the wildlings' arrival, calling out with hungry howls. From every side the dangers closed in on the Sem: the wolves' mountain ahead, the cold-hearted Mongauli following behind, and all around the perilous, tumbled rocks that held the prospect of attack by stone-mimics. And yet the wildlings had no choice but to trudge onward, holding back their misery in grim silence. How long could this march of terror continue?

"Gaulo."

Loto's voice was low, but its unusually sharp tone stopped the feet of the Sem.

"What is it? You cannot walk anymore because you are tired?" Gaulo spoke poisonously. "We will leave you here, then."

Loto raised his hand, his grizzled white face looking upwards.

"Don't you feel that something is not right?"

"What?"

Loto seemed hesitant to speak, but after a moment's indecision he said, "Have you noticed that the howling of the wolves just dropped off?"

Gaulo shrugged his shoulders irritably. "The pack must have moved to the far side of the mountain."

"No, I don't think so. Balto cries have also ceased. This area has become too quiet. Something is wrong."

Gaulo turned around and checked to make sure that the

Mongauli torches were still in the distance. "The *oh-mu* are coming behind us. We are getting close to Dog's Head Mountain. If the *oh-mu* could catch up with us, they would have already attacked us." Gaulo gave Loto a fierce look. "Instead of standing here and worrying about wolves' howling or not howling, why don't we hurry on and try to get to the mountain? Once we reach Dog's Head it will be safer—there is food and water there. The way up is right ahead. Let us hurry—"

"Ohh!"

Before Gaulo could finish speaking, the two chiefs' ears were smitten by the piercing cries of the Rasa, who were leading the way for the Sem force.

"*Oh-mu*!"

"*Oh-mu* were waiting for us!"

"Yeee-aaa!"

"Gaulo! Siba!" Loto's reaction was instantaneous. "It's a trap! Let's fight our way out! We will cut our way through the ambush!"

"That's impossible!" Kalto screamed. He seemed on the verge of weeping. "The Sem cannot fight anymore! We must escape! Esca..." He turned around, and his despairing voice trailed off. The Mongauli torches were moving more quickly now, and drawing closer.

"Look!"

Siba pointed to the foot of Dog's Head Mountain. Where until now there had been only shadow, lone torches had sprung to life and were moving like the ill-omened spirits of the dead, drawing strange figures in the darkness. With a feeling of dread the Sem realized that a force of Mongauli troops had placed a trap for them precisely where they intended to go; no doubt, those were signal fires communicating to the pursuing army that the Sem had been cornered.

"You bitches' spawn! You swine!" Gaulo roared at the half-seen enemy.

But the wildlings had no time to waste in outrage or stupefied shock. As suddenly as if it had risen from the ground, a Mongauli ambush unit had emerged to close off the path between the Sem and Dog's Head Mountain; meanwhile, the main force was catching up quickly from behind, their torches flickering like fireflies in the night.

"Loto!" Siba looked beseechingly at his aged chieftain, desperate for a plan of action.

"Keep calm. Be ready to hide behind the rocks as soon as the attack begins."

Loto spoke serenely, and in his tone was something that transformed the Sem around him from cornered mice to formidable warriors once again. The wildlings readied their quivers of poisoned darts and lifted their stone axes. They placed Loto, Suni, and the others who were badly injured in the center of their force, and faced outward in all directions to be ready for the first attack. Rough breathing filled the darkness, and whispered cries of "Alphetto!"

"Attack!"

Suddenly the shout of a young Mongauli captain broke the silence of the night. Horses were not useful in this rocky area, and the Mongauli had dismounted along the way and advanced on foot. The metallic sounds of their armor revealed their position as they moved.

"Ayee-yaa!"

Gaulo, Kalto, and Siba issued rough orders, and battle was joined in the darkness—a battle to the death, with no quarter given.

"Au-ah! Aiee, ayee-yaaa!"

"Alphetto! Alphetto!"

"Mongaul! Mongaul! Mongaul!"

The moon was hidden and the stars had vanished from the sky. In the total darkness amongst the crags, the clash of stone axes against helmets and steel swords created bursts of blue sparks that illuminated the grimacing teeth of ape-men and the raised blades of knights in sudden, eerie flashes.

"Don't lose them! Don't let them escape!"

"Kill them all!"

There was no difference now between the Karoi and the Raku—it was difficult even to distinguish between Mongauli and Sem. The knights advanced with outstretched hands, and if they touched hard, cold armor they pulled back, but if they felt warm bristly hair a swift sword stroke would follow. Screams, high-pitched death rattles, and the thrashing of mortal agony proclaimed the result.

Siba picked up Suni and pushed her into a hole in the shelter of a large rock, then hefted his axe and returned to the battle. Huddled miserably in the bleak, narrow place, Suni tried to shrink her tiny body still smaller; she curled into a ball, wishing that she could sink into the ground.

Then, with a sudden thud, a Mongauli soldier who had been fighting nearby tripped over the rock that protected Suni and fell into the hole beside her. Eyes that burned hungrily with the lust of battle spied the hairy creature with shining eyes that cowered at the bottom.

"Here is one more!"

Even as the soldier shouted in his thick voice he raised his sword and prepared to plunge it into the cowering wildling girl.

"Hiiieee!" Suni screamed—

And the soldier made a faint gurgling noise and toppled over on his side. This time, it was not the rock that had taken him off his feet. Suni's eyes grew round with surprise, and she tried to shrink deeper into the hole, but someone grabbed her roughly by her arms and pulled her out. Familiar eyes glinted at her from the darkness.

"Come on now, let's save Rinda and Remus," whispered Istavan. Then, tugging Suni along behind him, he made his way downhill from boulder to boulder.

The rocky area where the Sem had made their stand was illuminated now by a mass of torches that was drawing nearer along the path the wildlings had taken. The battle was clearly visible now; the Sem were fighting a desperate fight as one by one they were surrounded and killed. The stones resounded with their frantic growling, and the smell of blood filled the air as though it had leaked there from the oasis. It would only be a matter of time until all the Sem were slaughtered.

— 3 —

"Run for it!" a voice that sounded like Kalto's shrieked out, then changed abruptly to a growl and then a scream of pain, and was swallowed up by other screams.

"Loto!" Siba shouted, determined never to abandon the high chieftain or leave the old warrior unprotected. "Let's get out of here! I will cut us a path through the enemy line..."

The pursuing Mongauli force had arrived with fire and wrath at the rocky area where the Sem were making their stand. The soldiers had dismounted where the terrain made riding impossible, and now they approached on foot, each bearing a torch in one hand and a sword in the other. The new arrivals pushed forward between the high walls of the boulders to offer assistance to Astrias's men. This was a dangerous maneuver in that it halved their effective fighting capacity, but it allowed them to light the area brightly with their torches—a cruel dawn to reveal the Sem as they sought to hide among the rocks or flee under cover of darkness.

"Don't leave any alive this time—slit their throats if they try to escape!" Feldrik's shout pierced the darkness.

Vlon, who had ridden beside the Lady Amnelis during the entire chase, declared with a smile, "General, these are pitiful opponents, not even worthy of fighting."

"Do not call this a fight," Amnelis answered, her beautiful lips curled into a cruel smile. "This is a slaughter of beasts—just a monkey hunt."

Indeed, the contest could hardly be described as a battle. The Sem had finally lost their desire to fight. Abandoning any semblance of order, they became more monkey than human, and milled about wildly in a last ditch effort to survive. Despite the efforts of some of their leaders to marshal their forces, their followers tried only to escape, screaming fiercely and bumping into one another as they fled, hiding behind each other's bodies to avoid the sharp swords of the Mongauli. Most of those who remained alive were already drenched in the blood of their fellow Sem.

"Fight, fight!"

"Stand fast! Don't run!"

The commands of the chiefs were swallowed up by the shrieks of the others.

"Ayeeaaa!"

"Yeeee!"

As the Sem raced frantically back and forth, they collided and pushed each other to the ground and trod on their fallen fellows. The Mongauli were laughing as they chased after the monkey-folk; free now of the fear of battle, they had cast aside their helmets so they could breathe more freely and more easily see their victims. The tips of their swords shone red in the light of the torches, and the same flames illuminated the blood lust on their faces. The Mongauli troops were no longer satisfied with simply slaughtering the Sem; they had begun to play sadistic games using their vanquished foes. Horrible acts of violence were carried out everywhere.

"I will chop off this one's hands!"

"I will take the legs!"

"And I will take the eyes!"

The Mongauli cursed the fleeing wildlings and chased them with waving swords, competing to see who could cut off or gouge out named Sem body parts the quickest. One group caught a screaming ape-man and, purposely setting aside their swords, killed it instead by hitting it between the eyes with a heavy rock, crushing its face to a pulp even as it looked up at them in terror.

"Count Marus burned alive!" a soldier screamed, as red-faced as if he were drunk. "They will taste the same!"

He caught a Sem and doused its head with vasya oil, then ignited the fluid with the torch he carried in his other hand. A band of nearby soldiers laughed uproariously as the Sem became a fireball and rolled around screaming on the ground.

"How many *taal* will the next one go before it burns to death?"

"I will bet one raan on ten *taal*!"

"I will bet one raan and one bottle of honey wine on five!"

"Ten *taal*—I will wager my spare armor!"

Howling like fiends, the band went looking for other Sem that would be suitable for their game. The soldiers waved their torches as they ran after the wildlings, exchanging guesses about which ones would burn well, and favoring the ones with the thickest coats of fur.

In another area a bunch of soldiers had begun a contest to see who could cut off the head of a Sem and leave it hanging by the smallest flap of skin. When a neck was severed completely by mistake, a Mongauli clicked his tongue and kicked the head casually aside as if he were playing a game of Yan ball.

The Sem's monkeylike appearance had made it easy for the Gohran soldiers to fall into merry, unrestrained brutality. They gouged out Sem's eyes and peeled off their skin as casually as if they were killing dogs and cats. Some were cutting off only the tails of the wildlings, and piling them up into a heap. Some were laughing as they held down the poor little ape-men to pierce their arms and legs with their swords. Some took the Sem's poisoned darts and used the wildlings for target practice with their own weapons. There were heads without eyes, torsos without heads, arms without fingers, faces with the skin peeled off, gouged out eyes everywhere. Leaking brains, intestines, and blood flowed over the ground in a gruesome stream; the ground had become so slimy with offal that the soldiers needed to step carefully as they picked their way over the carcasses of their foes. The terrible reek of slaughter rose high into the air.

If the Mongauli had not been so focused on the violence they were wreaking, they would have noticed the shining blue eyes of wolves looking out from behind the rocks on all sides. The creatures were so excited by the smell of blood that they had lost their fear of fire, and watched with curled lips and drooling mouths. Fortunately for the soldiers the blood and meat of the fallen Sem were enough for all the wolves that lived on Dog's Head Mountain. The slavering canines slunk out quickly and seized carcasses and severed heads to drag back with them behind the rocks. The revolting sounds of bones being crushed and warm blood being lapped up were heard from all around.

"The last day of the Sem" was played out in a scene of living hell—and still the Mongauli were not sated with killing, but rampaged on, all semblance of discipline, self-control, and reason among them gone.

"Ohhhh!"

Nobody paid any attention to Rinda, who was screaming with horror as she clung tightly with both hands to Remus's shaking shoulders. The twins had been tied together at the ankles and forced to stand at an improvised cavalry hitching-post. Rinda's cheeks were wet with tears, and she was wretching repeatedly.

Ahead of her, the furry little simians she had known as happy and carefree were now screaming in pain and writhing in agony as they were slain by swords or held down to be skinned alive.

"Ohh...! How could this... Janos, Janos, have mercy!"

Rinda could not stop screaming. She clung tightly to her little brother's body, as if he could somehow save her, or return her from this nightmare to some less awful place.

"Ohhh... Please stop, stop!" she babbled, barely coherent. "What did they do to deserve this? What sin did they commit? This can't be!"

Glimpsed in the torchlight, the brutally slaughtered carcasses of the Sem began to overlap in her mind with the bloody tragedy that had befallen the noble folk of Parros in the Crystal Palace. To Rinda's eyes, the colors of the Mongauli's armor burned like a sigil of evil, and in her bewildered imagination the Sem who were dying in agony became her dear relatives and the people of her country.

"Stop," she groaned as though disgorging blood and buried her face against Remus's chest. *How could this be permitted? How could the gods let this be? Guin, why aren't you coming to help us, Guin!*

"Rinda."

She was so filled with sorrow and desperation that she was not aware of the low voice that had quietly spoken her name. Remus was the first one to take notice.

"Rinda!" the prince whispered anxiously, and nudged his sister.

Rinda raised her face in surprise. A red knight was standing nearby, gazing at both of them meaningfully. Through the visor of his helmet bright black eyes seemed to be sending them a secret message.

"I..." Rinda swallowed, unable to say more. A giddy wave of hope suddenly flooded her heart.

"I've been looking for you. You silly kids gave me a lot of trouble," Istavan of Valachia whispered to them with a suppressed smile. He casually resettled his helmet and glanced around to make sure the soldiers nearby were totally occupied with the slaughter. Then, concealing himself behind the horse that was tethered beside them, the mercenary bent down and cut the rope that secured the twins' ankles. As soon as he was finished, the two children tensed as if to bolt, but, before they could move, Istavan seized them by the arms.

"Don't run! You'll draw attention. Move slowly—just slip from behind this horse to the shelter of that boulder, and then keep going, from rock to rock. While they are busy—slowly, all right? You understand. Suni is hiding behind that rock over there. I told her to steal a horse. Lead it to where you can ride, and escape."

"Istavan, what are you going to do?"

"You don't have to worry about me. I'll take care of myself," Istavan declared self-consciously, as if he was determined to make up for slipping away from the oasis and leaving the twins behind. "All right, now—go!"

Rinda hesitated, intending to ask again what Istavan planned to do, but he put his hand over her mouth and pointed along the escape route he had chosen for them.

"I said, 'Go!' Keep your body low, crawl like a worm if you have to! Don't show your faces above the rocks. And don't waste time! It's almost sunrise. Once the sun is up, everything will be over."

"I-I understand."

Remus pulled at Rinda's hand as she continued to hesitate. At last she turned to follow him, but, even as they began to move, an exclamation from somewhere chillingly close stopped them short.

"Wait! What are you doing? Why did you cut the bindings of the twins?"

The severe voice made the twins shrink down in dismay. Istavan's whole body grew stiff.

Again the voice spoke commandingly.

"You are one of the red knights! Do you belong to Astrias Corps? What is your name? Or are you an agent of Parros?"

"No, not at all. There is a reason…" Istavan started to explain as he turned to face his interrogator, then whipped out his sword.

But that was exactly what his enemy expected. Istavan's foe, an experienced combatant, had drawn his own blade as soon as the mercenary had turned. Now the Valachian saw that his adversary wore fine white armor and a helmet with a captain's trailing tassel. The helmet's visor was up, revealing the serious, angular face of Feldrik.

"You are as dull-witted as you are inept!" the white knight exclaimed. "I will put you to the question in front of the lady!"

Feldrik was a famous master of the sword. With an artful feint he neutralized Istavan's pass and darted the tip of his blade forward to cut the bindings of Istavan's helmet, causing it to fly off the mercenary's head as he jerked back to avoid the blow.

Doalspit, he's good! Istavan cursed inwardly. An instant later the point of Feldrik's sword was at Istavan's throat.

"Your name! Who are you? Why did you release the twins of Parros?"

Istavan's eyes darted right and left, seeking some means of escape. Feldrik's hard face grew harder still.

"If you do not speak your name, I will put this sword right through you!"

The white knight pushed forward, and Istavan, panting, was forced back into a corner among the boulders, his face pale and contorted.

"Speak your name!"

Feldrik began to press the tip of his sword into Istavan's throat. Then—

"Ohhhh!"

A wave of sound washed over them as hundreds of Mongauli troops shouted in sudden amazement.

"What..."

Feldrik stiffened, momentarily distracted. The Crimson Mercenary didn't miss his chance, slipping away from the tip of his enemy's sword and putting distance between them with a quick handspring.

"Wait!"

Feldrik started to run after him, and then froze in mid-step. His mouth fell open, and his eyes stared in disbelief at what he saw. By the look of surprise that spread across his features, he was afraid he was losing his sanity.

"Wh-" his mouth moved unconsciously, leaking a faint sound. "What is it?" he managed at last. The same words were repeated as screams from many Mongauli mouths.

"Ohh!"

The long and bloody night of slaughter was drawing to a close, and the sun was rising over Dog's Head Mountain, shining indifferently as if it knew nothing of the inhumanity in the world. The scene it illuminated with its yellow-gray light was like an image from the depths of Hell. The lights of the torches were suddenly subdued to smoky flames, as faint as the glow of fireflies before a great bonfire. The entire mountainside had become a spectacle of misery and brutal cruelty. Blood, freshly severed heads, entrails, brains—and in the midst of this, all who remained alive, whether Mongauli or Sem, commander or common soldier, were gaping uncomprehendingly at a point higher up on the slopes. Like the citizens of Kanan as they were changed to stone by the legendary witch Cyclope—with jaws dropped and fighting forgotten, they stood staring in wide-eyed shock. Rinda felt her heart leap with amazement.

"Gu..."

At last a voice—and, until it sounded, not one among them

had moved. Some grasped their bloody swords, and some stood poised to strike a blow, but they were all frozen by what they saw. They *could* not move.

"Guin..."

"Guin—"

"Guin!!"

Then the cry of this first voice spread like a ripple—like an echo sounding deep in the mountains and growing and multiplying among crooked crags.

"Guin!"

"Riyaad!"

"Riyaaaaaad!!"

Siba was the first to move. As if seized by a sudden madness he began to run, uncaring that his eyes were flowing with tears. A moment later Rinda also jumped up and ran toward the figure of the leopard-man, now visible in the growing light. Remus followed close behind her.

"Guin!" The name burst from Rinda's mouth like a sob. "Guin... Oh, Guin. Guin!"

It was as if her screams and her careless, headlong movement had lifted a curse from the frozen men. The baffled lull of silence became an ear-splitting din as the Mongauli soldiers expressed their disbelief, and the few remaining Sem cried out in joy.

"From where...where in the world did he..."

"What *is* that? What..."

"Guin..."

"Riyaad! Riyaaaad!"

The shouts of the Sem blended into a single enormous cheer.

"Riyaad! Riyaad! Riyaad!"

At the same time, the Mongauli voices began to falter as their minds struggled with the impossible sight before them. High above the battlefield, on the slope of Dog's Head Mountain where a broad crag jutted out from the surrounding rocks, the muscular leopard-headed warrior was standing with both arms folded across his chest, surveying the catastrophe through his mask of yellow and black as if he were an incarnation of the god of destiny controlling the world's vicissitudes.

On either side of him stood a group of magnificent giants larger than the leopard-man himself.

The giants had the look of fighters, fearless as the stalwart troops of the gods when the hero Cirenos led them, and just as valiant. The awe-inspiring sight was made even more unearthly by the fact that the giants' numbers were steadily increasing—the towering figures seemed to appear from nowhere, like the soldiers of Valgos who were said to spring forth from dragons' teeth hurled to the ground. One after another they stepped forward and formed up behind Guin. The ever-growing divine army was wrapped in the glory of the morning light at its back. The giants were marvelous in their shining beauty. Their soft-hued manes and the fine, downy hair that covered their bodies illuminated by the backlight of the sun, they looked almost translucent, or as if they emitted a hot light of their own. In their big hands they held heavy cudgels, and their hips were girded tightly with thick wolf-hide belts.

One figure, the biggest and most striking of them all—a veritable giant among giants—stood just behind Guin with his arms crossed upon his chest, glowering like Balbas, guard of Cirenos. Below his narrow brow and severe scowl the great giant's eyes were shining with a fire that seemed capable of burning down anything.

"Lagon..."

"Lagon—"

"Lagon!"

As their initial shock faded, the Mongauli realized the astounding truth: they were looking at a tribe of phantoms, long regarded as the merest legend, coming to life in front of their eyes.

Guin's hand rose up very slowly. He was grasping something strange, an object that shone a bright silver in the sunlight.

The mouth of the leopard gaped open. From within, an earth-moving, gut-shaking roar issued forth: "Sem—

"Sem!"

"Sem!!"

The giants were chanting in chorus. The earth rang.

Then, with Guin at their head, the Lagon began their charge down, their footfalls causing the very stones of Dog's Head Mountain to tremble.

—4—

"Soldiers of Mongaul!"

Urgent commands were streaming from the throats of the Mongauli orderlies; the situation had changed completely from the careless slaughter of a few moments before.

"Stand firm! These are dangerous enemies. Trust in your training! Use your skill, and fight with caution!"

"Don't be afraid! The enemy is greatly outnumbered."

"Reorganize the ranks! All troops, form battle lines immediately! We must not face the enemy in disorder. When they draw near, let three of our soldiers attack each one of them."

Only a few twists remained before the sun would rise completely. Amnelis was nearly in a frenzy, sending out messenger after messenger with orders intended to renew the fighting spirit of Mongaul. Vlon and Lindrot were dashing around in desperation, trying to reorganize the troops for battle. Once an army lost order, it became fragile; the more overwhelming the army's might and advantage and the greater its confidence, the more severe its fall when that confidence was sapped. The courage that the Mongauli forcibly mustered by telling themselves that these were merely large barbarians crumbled the moment the roaring giants came loping down to the boulders.

The Lagon were magnificent warriors, a tribe born for battle and trained to a life of war. Each was an expert in the use of the swords and the heavy cudgels they favored, and even unarmed they were extremely formidable; their massively built bodies were not only large but agile and supple as well.

The Mongauli fought hard, but just as the Sem were no match for them, so were the humans easily overwhelmed by the Lagon. The rocky slopes of the mountains were the Lagon's home. Their hard feet stepped lightly over the stones like the hooves of antelope. When their enormously strong arms lifted high and swung their weapons, Mongauli heads flew right and left, and decapitated bodies fell and vomited forth blood until the ground was dyed crimson.

"This is more like it!"

Istavan had hurriedly removed his stolen armor and helmet and resumed his light attire to avoid being confused with the Mongauli, and he had rejoined the fray, fighting adroitly. His voice had taken on a jovial tone as he bantered between sword-thrusts, admiring the imposing Lagon and talking more to

himself than to anyone else.

"What a great fighting style they have! They certainly know how to use a sword. Especially the biggest one—he is fighting like Ruah! I'd give a lot to see a match between him and Guin! These are the allies we needed all along. I wonder where—and how—Guin found 'em? Good old Guin... Oh, I swear on the nymph who mothered Cirenos, this is the greatest display of fighting skill I have ever seen! I'm sure glad these giants are on our side. I doubt I'd survive for very long against them!"

While Istavan rambled on, he was demonstrating his own fighting prowess, airily sidestepping enemy attacks and jumping high as he slashed and parried. Feldrik, meanwhile, was rushing to escape from this sudden reversal of fortunes.

"Wait, you coward!" Istavan shouted merrily, darting after the white knight and extending his blade in a wicked thrust. Feldrik screamed and toppled forward as he ran. A band of Mongauli rushed to protect their captain, some closing ranks to block Istavan's attack, others pulling Feldrik to his feet and helping him away.

"Oh! I almost forgot..." Istavan abruptly stopped short, his joviality gone. *I shouldn't show my face.* Warily he watched as Feldrik was taken away. His first impulse was to try to catch up and finish him, but the Valachian soon talked himself out of it. "Ah, why risk it? He's old—with that wound he won't last long."

Making this assumption he began to work his way toward Guin and his force of Lagon, all the while taking care not to reveal his distinctive face.

The Sem, too, wasted no time now that they had such powerful allies.

"Riyaad's reinforcements are here! Rise up and fight, Sem!"

"Riyaad, Riyaad!"

"Don't get separated! Gather together, and fight against the *oh-mu* as one troop!"

Although they had suffered terrible losses in the merciless night battle with the Mongauli, the diminutive desert warriors didn't retreat to nurse their injuries while their powerful new allies took the lead. Instead, all the Sem who had survived now gathered around their chiefs, encouraging one another with fierce, piercing screams. As soon as the battle was joined again, they rushed forward, brave and heedless as ever, treading over their fallen fellows' carcasses as they charged. With the tables turned, the Sem's naturally brutal character was now given full scope to be displayed; gone were the helpless victims who had been chased, tortured to death, and subjected to countless atrocities just moments before.

"Let us take revenge for our comrades!"

"Don't stay back behind the Lagon!"

"Aiieee, yeeee!"

The Sem flung themselves against the Mongauli lines and attacked like ants savaging a butterfly while the Lagon swung their massive cudgels with terrifying strength. Where the Sem's poison-tipped darts flew between the longswords, Mongauli warriors clutched at their eyes and fell to the ground, screaming in blind agony. Where the Lagon's heavy weapons struck home, metal helmets and armor crushed as though made of flimsy paper, and Mongauli soldiers were literally knocked into pieces, reduced in one blow to ragged masses of muddy blood, shattered organs, and fragments of red bone.

Even in the headlong confusion of the melee, the superb fighting prowess of Dodok the Brave and the leopard-headed Guin stood out and drew attention. Wherever these two headed the Mongauli quickly cleared away. Dodok's rock hard arms could snatch up running soldiers as though they were ambling puppies, and in his grasp their bodies broke like straw in the grip of a storm. With his heavy cudgel he brushed aside the longswords of the brave knights who summoned the courage to stand and fight him, and in the next moment, he smashed their heads as they stood frozen in fear with eyes white and staring. It was not for nothing that Dodok the Brave was called the strongest among all the mighty warriors of the Lagon.

And Guin...

"You! You, Guin!" Astrias snarled through clenched teeth. "Fight with me! Stand and face me! I have been looking for you!"

He was striving to reach Guin even as he fended off the attacks of several Lagon warriors. Pollak, following close behind him, was frantically trying to persuade his captain to stop.

"This is madness, sir! That creature is not human! He must be a god or a demon, with that horrible leopard's head! Do you want to die? Captain!"

"I don't care if he is a god, or a demon, or Doal himself..."

"Look at how he fights!" Pollak panted.

"I want to challenge him!"

"Don't die in a place like this!"

Astrias turned away from his lieutenant to shout again into the midst of the battle. "Guin, fight with me! With me, Guin!"

A sudden thought occurred to Pollak. "Captain! We have a duty to protect our lady. We must fall back to protect our Lady of Mongaul's banner."

"Our Lady of Mongaul..."

Astrias's eyes opened wide. With a shake of his head he came to his senses and gazed back towards the place where his cherished lady had established her command post. He cursed silently at what he saw. The raging Lagon were approaching the post and Amnelis's personal guard. Their immaculate figures dyed with blood, the white knights, who until then had rarely entered into the fray of battle themselves, strove desperately to drive back the incoming giants.

"Lady Amnelis is in danger!" Astrias shouted. He spun around to address the red knights in formation behind him. "Troops, change direction! Reinforce the Lady General's guard!"

"It's about time," muttered Pollak, whose true obsession was to protect his young captain.

"Pull back, pull back! Protect Lady Amnelis!" Astrias bellowed his orders. He could not fail to notice Guin, who was trampling over Irrim Corps as though berserk; yet he resolutely turned from the hated foe and headed for the lady-general. It was no easy task to reach her, however. The bulk of the Lagon force was now between them. Astrias clenched his teeth and charged forward, swinging his sword like a madman, but against that formidable barrier he made little progress—it was like swimming against a flood tide. In the meantime, the troops of white knights, with little time to reform their ranks, faced a difficult fight.

"My lady!" Vlon came running from amidst the fray. "My lady, we are at a disadvantage here. Let us withdraw for the time being. Please, give the order to retreat!"

"What are you saying, Vlon?!" Amnelis twisted her slender

hands together. Her voice was vehement. "We have come this far at last, and you suggest retreat? This is just an action against savages—and we are the army of Mongaul! Our superb soldiers cannot show their backs to mere barbarians!"

"Those giants..." Vlon was at a loss for words.

Gajus stood up slowly. "My lady, please order the drums to sound a withdrawal."

"Gajus! You, too?" Amnelis pushed back her blond hair irritably. "Or are you merely saying that we need only withdraw from this place for the time being, due to unfavorable terrain—that we shall trounce these creatures later at a battlefield of our choosing? *That* I could understand, Gajus."

"I am suggesting that the whole invasion force return to the banks of the River Kes and beyond to our defensive walls," Gajus replied brusquely.

Amnelis held her breath, growing pale with vexation, and stared at both Gajus and Vlon. She drew herself up to her full height. But before she could speak again, a voice cried out wildly from nearby—

"Lady! Beware!"

A Lagon warrior had burst through the double and treble lines of protection and was closing in on them with his enormous cudgel held high. At the sight of him Amnelis froze and screamed with fear. With a shout of dismay Vlon sprang forward and pushed her aside. The next instant, the heavy cudgel hit Vlon across the side; he staggered sideways with a gasp and spun half way around before he struck the ground, where he convulsed, vomited globs of blood, and lay still. An instant later the Lagon who had killed him was cut in half from behind by a mighty stroke of Lindrot's sword. He, too, had returned to suggest a retreat.

"Lady, it is very dangerous here! Let us return to the River Kes to regroup and join with Ricard's forces."

Amnelis stood as though in shock, looking as pale and fragile as a piece of paper. She nodded without speaking. Gajus and Lindrot took up protective positions on either side of her and hurriedly withdrew from the field of battle. Soon, a Mongauli drum could be heard sounding the retreat, echoing into the clear dawn sky.

"General withdrawal! The army will retreat to the banks of the River Kes!"

"Withdraw! Withdraw!"

Lindrot helped Amnelis astride her horse, wishing he could comfort her. When he looked into her face, words failed him. Her cheeks were drawn and her visage ghostly, and she bit her lip as she surveyed the battle unraveling around her. She had lost the notorious proud bearing of the Lady of Mongaul—even her famed blond hair seemed to have faded and lost its brightness. Suddenly Amnelis looked her age, as if she were indeed an ordinary, powerless and frail eighteen-year-old maiden. Around her the renowned fighting men of her archduchy leaped onto their horses without waiting to reform their ranks, rushing to escape to the west and the distant sanctuary of the Kes. The magnificence of their bearing when they had last crossed the river was nowhere in sight.

The Mongauli expeditionary force of fifteen thousand strong had been reduced to a pitiful remnant one third that number. The beat of the drum sounding the retreat rose like a cry of despair, a final proof of the broken aspirations of the Mongauli to seize control of Nospherus and to learn its secrets.

"The rear guard...?"

Amnelis finally regained sufficient composure to pose the question only after the army had withdrawn from the rocky slopes below Dog's Head Mountain and ridden pell-mell all the way back through the war-torn oasis. She had just been informed that the mixed force of Lagon and Sem that had assailed them no longer posed an imminent threat.

"Astrias Corps is on duty," Lindrot answered heavily.

"Astrias...is safe?" Amnelis looked like she wanted to say more, but she stopped. "How about Gajus?"

Gajus, too, was accounted for, but—

"We cannot find Cal Moru," Lindrot informed her sullenly.

"What do you mean?" Amnelis demanded anxiously. The loss of the spellcaster would be a great blow to the Mongauli cause. Without Cal Moru of Kitai, the Mongauli could never hope to find the great secret hidden at the heart of Nospherus. "He has fallen into their hands?"

"Somebody saw him get cut down. He cannot be alive."

"I see..."

Amnelis's perfect features took on a look of bleak resignation. She whispered to herself:

A thorough disaster... What to tell my father?

This was the first time Amnelis had ever been defeated, the first time she had been forced to withdraw her forces from the field of battle. She swallowed a hot lump rising in her throat. In the passionate determination of her eighteen years she found the loss almost too much to accept as fact. And Guin—that leopard-headed monstrosity who had turned her around so easily and robbed her of all but certain victory—him she didn't even have the energy to curse and hate right now.

Yet she knew very well that she would never forget his name or his freakish figure. Though her defeated troops, straggling home through the sands, would see and hear, Amnelis buried her face in her horse's mane and gave herself up to weak, drawn-out sobs.

The Kes River was still hundreds of tads away. The desert,

filled with a feeling of brooding hostility, hungrily spread its white expanse before the crushed army.

The battle for Nospherus was over.

"Riyaad!"

Siba ran up to Guin and, throwing himself at the leopard-man's feet, wept.

A moment later Dodok arrived. "Riyaad, shouldn't we chase after them and kill them all?" asked the giant.

"We have done enough," Guin stayed him. "Mongaul's plans for Nospherus have been ripped to shreds. They should now turn their eyes once again to the Middle Country, but were they to plan another invasion, with the Lagon as its protectors Nospherus is safe from the trampling feet of Mongaul. Dodok, the Lagon are certainly a tribe made for fighting."

Guin's laugh was a roar.

With long strides Guin stalked down the middle of the battlefield, tiny Siba and giant Dodok keeping pace on either side. All around them the Sem were busy finishing off wounded Mongauli, cutting their throats with blades of stone. Bodies from both forces were piled on top of one another everywhere, and the air was filled with the smell of blood and death, a scene of nightmare illuminated by the bright light of the desert sun.

Suddenly Guin stopped short. His eyes took on a look of

strange surprise, and he stared down at a shape before his feet.

"Riyaad?"

Siba and Dodok looked down dubiously, and Dodok frowned.

"What is this monster? It has yet to be eaten by sand leeches but already has the form of a death's head!"

The three were gazing upon a carcass garbed in a black, deeply hooded mantle. The hood had fallen aside, revealing a terrible, otherworldly face that had melted down shapelessly to expose deep eye sockets and a skeletal jaw.

The figure's chest had been skewered brutally from behind by a Lagon spear which remained there. Cal Moru, who had survived walking across the desert of Nospherus, who had returned from the Valley of Death, could not elude the peril brought to him by the Lagon. His crippled form had no longer commanded any magic. His thin, bony wrists, ending in handless stumps, were stretched out as though he were pleading for help. A single eyeball remained in one of his black eye sockets, staring emptily up at the sky.

The three companions left the spot without saying anything more. They did not and could not know that the secret of Gur Nuu—the Valley of Death that made Nospherus into a land of death and a home of monsters—had surfaced for a while like some vessel just to plunge deeper into the netherworld with the passing of Cal Moru. Many years were to elapse before the resurgence of the secret and still more before its elucidation.

The three warriors were unmoved by the carnage as they walked on through the field of battle. Often their feet almost slipped on the bloody guts spilled upon the ground; all around them carcasses were drying out and stiffening under the sun. Severed heads, arms, and trunks of bodies were everywhere. Some of the Sem were satisfying their hunger by eating dead men. Shortly after the three passed by a spot where the bodies lay thickest, they heard voices calling.

"Guin!"

"Oh, Guin!"

Two children were running towards them, almost falling down in their haste.

"Rinda! Remus!"

Guin let the two crying children cling to him on either side. Their bodies heaved with sobs of relief.

"Oh, Guin, Guin, Guin! I always believed in you. I believed that you would come back to save us. I knew that you would take care of everything! I believed in you, always..."

Rinda's voice trailed off into more sobs; the tears were running in streams down her grimy face. Guin's big, trustworthy hands gripped the shoulders of the royal twins who had lost their country.

"I would have come back earlier, if I could."

His voice was warm and soothing.

"It's a good thing you two came here with the Sem when you did. The Lagon know of a limestone cavern called the Wind Hole that passes through Dog's Head, leading from one side of the mountain to the other. We took that path. I was growing a little desperate thinking about the distance to the battlefield. I did not know how close to me the battlefield had moved! When I saw the end of the Wind Hole and heard the sound of fighting, I thought it must be a dream. At the same time, I became convinced that the heavens are on our side."

"Oh, Guin!" was all Rinda could say.

The leopard warrior continued his inspection of the battlefield with the twins clinging to him as though he might disappear again. They had not gone much farther when they heard a loud yell from between some boulders. Siba rushed forward to investigate and was surprised to discover Istavan, the Crimson Mercenary, with his back pressed up against a rock. Unmoved by the Valachian's protests, a Lagon was about to swing his heavy cudgel down at the head of the human survivor.

Guin halted the Lagon just in time and told him who Istavan was. The Valachian roared with anger.

"What a farce! I fought so hard in this cursed battle, and after all my efforts, I nearly get killed by my own ally! What kind of an ally is that? Doal's dung, Guin! Do you always have to bring with you monsters, nincompoops, and bloodthirsty sandworm kin?"

Rinda and Remus looked at each other. Rinda felt a spark of anger at the mercenary's words and was about to upbraid him for his ungratefulness, but after a moment, realizing the absurdity of the situation, she burst out laughing instead. The sight of Istavan's angry face and wide open eyes suddenly seemed downright comical. They were still alive. After all they had been through, that was enough to fill the twins with a happiness warm and sweet as sunshine.

The party continued onward with the addition of Istavan. They soon arrived at the bottom of the rocky slope, where Loto and most of the other Sem warriors who had survived the terrible battle were awaiting them.

"Hey!" Istavan called out merrily, forgetting that the wildlings did not understand his language. He gave them an exaggerated wink. "Lovely weather, eh?"

"Riyaad..." Loto lifted both his arms as if he were a legendary hermit in miniature, a giver of blessings. "And Lagon... the Sem's friends..."

"Siba!" Guin turned to the wildling warrior who walked beside him.

"Yes, Riyaad?"

"Ask the surviving Sem to gather by tribe, and survey them to find out how much damage each tribe has suffered."

"Yes, Riyaad."

"Dodok."

"Yes?"

"It is time that our little friends the Sem meet the warriors of the Lagon. Can you gather your folk here?"

"I will do that."

Guin watched as the two hurried away, and then he went to stand beside Loto and laid his big hand softly on the old Sem's shoulder and nodded to himself several times. Loto looked up at him in silence. A few paces away, Rinda and Remus were crying quietly with joy at their reunion. Little Suni was snuggled between the two of them, chirping away despite her painful head wound. Although the twins still struggled with her language, it was clear what she was saying.

"Alra ye em Alphetto."

"That is right, Suni." Rinda held the little Sem girl, who kept talking excitedly. "You are still alive—that is good. That is really good. Everything is fine now—everything is safe. The killing is over. Nospherus is protected; Guin protected it. And the Sem and the Lagon did, too."

Remus gazed out over the desert pensively, wondering if the Mongauli had really given up. Would they not build up their strength again and bare their fangs? Not today, perhaps, but tomorrow? The young prince was careful not to mouth his thoughts—not now.

"Riyaad!"

"Guin, I have gathered them."

Siba and Dodok had returned. Guin nodded, and with Rinda, Remus, Suni, and Istavan following close behind, went to them.

"What are the Sem's losses?" the leopard-man inquired.

Siba's face clouded.

"They are very great. The Tubai are almost annihilated—but I think they will be able to pull through." A fierce light flashed in his eyes, and all at once his energy returned. "The Sem have survived through much harder years. The Sem are a very strong race. We are small, but we have big, strong hearts. The Sem will be all right."

"Yes, I know that to be true." Guin nodded. "The Sem are warriors. The Sem protected Nospherus."

"And Riyaad protected the Sem." Loto spoke very slowly as he made his way to stand at the front of the Sem throng.

Then, as the royal heirs of Parros looked on, Guin oversaw the formal meeting of the surviving Sem, led by Loto, and the giant Lagon, led by Kah the Wise; and the two wildling races of Nospherus swore friendship to each other. When Loto and

Kah exchanged their oaths, the shouts of joy from the throats of the gathered wildlings echoed up to shake the very crags of Dog's Head Mountain.

The unlikely alliance presented a fantastic spectacle: on one side, Dodok the Brave and Kah the Wise, with his paralyzed legs, at the head of a mighty battalion of giants who stood two *taal* in height and weighed one hundred and fifty *skones*; on the other, the hairy Sem with their stone axes, no taller than children, assembled behind high chieftain Loto of the Raku tribe and brave young Siba. Between these two forces loomed the enigmatic warrior Guin, his arms crossed upon his chest, looking like a figure of legend with his powerful dark body and strange feline countenance. The clear blue of the desert sky and the bright sandy waves of the dunes surrounded them; the platinum blond heads of Rinda and Remus shone in the sun.

"Riyaad," Siba asked hesitantly, "what if the *oh-mu* come to attack us again?"

"With the Sem and the Lagon united together, the humans cannot win. Nospherus belongs to the tribes of Nospherus."

Guin laughed. Then he mumbled as if he'd just remembered:

"Only, I have to bring my fight with Dodok to an end."

"And if you beat me, you will be the next Dodok the Brave," Dodok noted with apparent enthusiasm.

Guin shook his head.

"Riyaad, what are you going to do now?" Loto asked, speaking slowly.

"I have not decided."

"If you would become King of Nospherus and govern both the Lagon and the Sem..."

Guin looked down at him in surprise, and then gazed around at the Sem and the Lagon. Every face was smiling and nodding. Guin started to laugh.

"That might be good. I—love this desert."

The blue sky and the desert dunes heard the great shout of joy that greeted these words. Rinda brought her hands softly together.

Guin, the leopard-headed warrior. When he appeared in the Roodwood he was but a wanderer, utterly alone. Now he had friends, the Lagon and the Sem.

End of Book Five

and of

The Marches Episode

Afterword

THE AGE OF CHAOS

Listen—

I tell of an age before that long Nothing when time and space lost all who might measure them. Just as there are none who can tell us of the Nothing, all that came before it, too, is a memory that exists only in legends and tales turned half to myth.

Yet it existed, without question, this history; already then, man bravely struggled to raise the precarious torch of civilization and sagacity against the primitive darkness that had enveloped his prehistory for an unspeakably long period.

Nay, if any age was ever truly wise, perhaps that was the only one—not because man mastered so much, from the genesis of the cosmos, to the means of traveling far and high, to the means of perceiving two worlds, both the infinitely large and the infinitesimally small, but rather because, as those who speak of the age always say of it: "In those days, man was wiser than he is now, for he understood that he knew some things but not others. Moreover, he knew what things he must not know and what things he did not need to know."

At any rate it was not the "primitive age" that we have come to call it. Science existed, and so did that which we term the scientific spirit. Yet, just as the common man did not concern himself with the principles by which the sorcerer wielded his spells, so too did the same possess sufficient wisdom to leave scientific matters to a minority of scholars, neither troubling them nor in turn troubled by them.

In that age, man lived in a society where classes and taboos were firmly established but he did not feel fettered by them, since it was what he chose, and ample opportunities still existed to exit it. As in any age and society, outsiders formed a society of their own, large numbers joining the strata of mercenaries, itinerants, bards, caravaners and prostitutes. While citizens treated them as outsiders, the boundary itself was tenuous and hence all of it a matter not so much of discrimination as of mere distinction. The citizens accepted the existence of an outsider society with its own rules just as they accepted that there were lords; that there were magi; that there were great men, although their numbers were truly few; and that these had their own rules. *So it is and so be it*—that, then, was something of a golden rule of the age.

It was an age when light and darkness, intellect and emotion, and sagacity and ignorance mixed indiscriminately; an age when science and sorcery, order and disorder, superstition and understanding, tyranny and largess, and arrogance and servility all freely asserted their rights; an age when man was as convinced of what is close to the gods as he was in awe of the magical realm.

It is true of any age, but especially of the one in question, that capturing it in one word is difficult. There was glory, yes, but blackness as well, savagery and war alongside peace and prosperity. If the age were to be spoken of in severance from the rest of history, then, more so than any other, it may appear to us a period of contradiction itself. For this reason, it was also a period when the true shape of things was thrown up awfully near to man together with so much worthless dross.

Historically, the age is called a tumultuous one. Many mighty realms rose, fell, and revived, or perished. The world did not belong to any one or a few ideals, or banners, nor did it belong to any one man. Every country, every king, every ideal and every accord carried secretly the awareness that it could never become absolute—gods and their servants included.

Lands vied against one another, annexed and were annexed. Kings lived in danger not only of assassination but also of crises of nonconfidence among their subjects. Sacred but not unassailable—a fundamental beauty of this age, or perhaps a sacrilege, which in any case applied to the gods as well—royalty attracted much adoration, only as long as it was merited.

Anything, any event, had the right to demand that it take place: coup d'état, dark reign, assassination, conspiracy, oppression, magnanimity, massacre and treachery, the base and the exalted, fanaticism, revolution, catastrophe, freedom and enslavement, and even the stern work of justice. It was a simple age, yet one filled with power, of the chaos that admits all, the age of that only truly glorious thing which is contradiction, and which is becoming lost to us if it is not already lost.

Naturally, there was a place for heroes, too. Their history was shaped, alongside that of scoundrels and assassins, by great emperors and warlords with sharp blades.

The Age of the Three Kingdoms, so-called, when the three powerful realms of Parros, Gohra, and Cheironia took center stage, each waxing and waning in strength, swallowing smaller lands about them, now dominating the Middle Country, now beating bitter retreats—this age whose contours we today are permitted if only vaguely to trace boasted a myriad of heroes.

It was the last age when one could become as great as the reach of his will, or as puny. In this sense, the age constituted the final act of the epoch of myth. The holy kings, warlords, princesses, tyrants, and strategists who became its players are too numerous to name. There was Holy King Alcandross, the founder of Parros; the warlord Vladislav of Mongaul; Yuro, aspirant to the throne; Archduke Vlad, who instigated the First

War of the Black Dragon; the *Magne* of Cheironia, Achilleus; the vampire emperor, Kolura Talus; the martyr Radu the Elder and his son, Duke Radu the Younger of Valachia; Sylvia, the traitor-princess who brought temporary ruin to Cheironia—and of course, the Gohran King Istavan the Usurper, and Holy King Remus, restorer of the Third Holy Kingdom of Parros. And finally, there was that hero of heroes, he who abandoned Cheironia, the mighty leopard-headed King Guin.

If we were to track the greatest and brightest "living myth" among the threads that wove this age of heroic tales, it would surely be that of the leopard-headed king of Cheironia. From nowhere he appeared, and walked into the annals of history.

It was his very emergence—or, to be more accurate, the events leading to his emergence—that marked the boundary between the years of tumult when small nations rose and fell and the later Age of the Three Kingdoms, when it was determined who would bestride the center stage and who would support from the skirts. In this sense he was both the last mythical hero and the first historical individual.

Always above him loomed both dawn and twilight. He was born from the chaos of the Age of Chaos but was also the first to intend order for it.

And this he did by ever seeking whence he had come.

THE GUIN SAGA *Manga*

The Seven Magi

ILLUSTRATED BY
KAZUAKI YANAGISAWA
STORY BY
KAORU KURIMOTO

Volume One
978-1932234-80-0

Many years after awaking in the Roodwood, the leopard-headed warrior has become King of Cheironia. Only he can dispel the black plague that ravishes his realm.

A three-volume manga based on the first *gaiden* side story of the saga. Ages 16 and up.

Volume Two
978-1-934287-07-1

Volume Three
978-1-934287-08-8